The Ninth Armada Gh

To
Lisa
from
Joanne.

Happy 11th Birthday July 1985

This Armada book belongs to:
Lisa J. Homer
102 New Street
Quarry Bank
C\H 65923

The Ninth Armada Ghost Book

Edited by Mary Danby

Illustrated by Peter Archer

The Ninth Armada Ghost Book was first
published in the U.K. in 1977 by
Fontana Paperbacks,
8 Grafton Street, London W1X 3LA.

This impression 1984.

The arrangement of this collection is copyright
© Mary Danby 1977

Printed in Great Britain by
William Collins Sons & Co. Ltd, Glasgow.

CONTENTS

ACKNOWLEDGEMENTS

The editor gratefully acknowledges permission to reprint copyright material to the following:

Guy Weiner and Michael Bakewell & Associates Ltd. for THE LAST FARE © Guy Weiner 1977.

Catherine Gleason for HOUSE OF GLASS © Catherine Gleason 1976.

Rosemary Timperley and Harvey Unna & Stephen Durbridge Ltd. for THE MURDEROUS GHOSTS © Rosemary Timperley 1977.

Sydney J. Bounds for THE HAUNTED CIRCUS © Sydney J. Bounds 1977.

Diana Pullein-Thompson for A STAR FOR A LADY © Diana Pullein-Thompson 1977.

Daphne Froome for LISA © Daphne Froome 1977.

John Duncan for CHILD OF THE FUTURE © John Duncan 1977.

Rick Ferreira and Campbell Thomson & McLaughlin Ltd. for THE PHANTOM PIRATES © Rick Ferreira 1977.

Margaret Biggs for GOODBYE, CHARLOTTE © Margaret Biggs 1977.

THE VACKIE is © Mary Danby 1977.

Introduction

IF you are on your own, and you see a ghost, you might be accused of having a too-vivid imagination. But if several people see the same ghost at the same time, what then? Is it mass-hallucination, or is the ghost they see a real, external presence, visible to each of them?

In *The Last Fare*, Harry says to his brother: "Two people can't have the same illusions at the same time. Or can they?" However, events show that the sight of Tiggy the cabman is more than just a shared memory from their childhood.

Tiggy is definitely a friendly ghost, unlike the dancing phantom that haunts Aunt Natalie's attic. She is both tragic and sinister, trying to ensnare Millie in her *House of Glass*.

Not menacing at all—except to each other—are Gregory and Annabel, *The Murderous Ghosts*. They claim to have killed each other, but Jack thinks it is all a joke—at first . . .

In *The Haunted Circus*, Charley the phantom clown, hovering helpfully beside Dianne, is no joke at all. Mind you, he does help her in the end—if not in the way she expected.

A Star for a Lady is not for the squeamish. It's the gruesome story of a wicked, cruel horse dealer who is paid back for his evil ways. But there's a kind, gentle ghost to follow—a clever cat, who leads *Lisa* to safety when she finds herself trapped in an empty house.

Another empty house is the setting for *Child of the Future*. However, as Rebecca is alarmed to discover, it is not entirely uninhabited . . .

Many miles away, on a Caribbean island, Captain Skull and *The Phantom Pirates* are up to their terrifying tricks, and Christopher is in mortal danger when he finds a Spanish doubloon—and keeps it.

Goodbye, Charlotte is the touching story of two lonely girls, linked across nearly a century by their bond of sad-

7

ness. And John, in *The Vackie*, is also haunted by unhappiness—in the strangest piece of homework he's ever sat down to write.

A chilling clutch of spooks and spectres, each with a quite different personality. Are they illusions? Or are they as real as the pages of this book? I leave you to decide for yourselves.

MARY DANBY

THE LAST FARE

by Guy Weiner

To remember the hansom cab that used to ply for hire outside Baron's Court Underground station, one must be at least as old as I am, and I've been retired now for five years.

It was a very old cab even then, with its well-polished varnish cracked and crinkled by the sun and rain, and its rubber tyres wore down almost to the rims of the wheels.

It used to stand there by the kerb waiting for the station to disgorge travellers, with old Tiggy Smith sitting up on the box, his ancient, grimy bowler hat square on his head and a horse blanket wrapped around his legs.

"Keb sir—keb sir," he would mutter mechanically at the passing throng. And occasionally, very occasionally, some tired traveller or overloaded shopper would take the cab. Tiggy Smith would shake the reins at the horse, and the cab would rattle its way down the cobbled slope towards Talgarth Road and beyond.

That was many years ago, before they made the clearway to London Airport and widened Talgarth Road by pulling down all the houses on one side.

Just a memory of when I lived as a child in nearby Edith Road. But one evening recently, I was playing chess with my brother at his flat at Chiswick when he said casually: "I see that the old hansom cab is back at Baron's Court station." Then the whole scene came flooding back to me.

"And I suppose it's still got 'Enery the 'orse pulling it, and Tiggy Smith on the box," I said as I took his second bishop.

He began to laugh at my remark, but the laugh died away.

"You know," he said slowly, "it was just like old Tiggy

as I remember him. And the horse had one white fetlock, like Henry had. It's really very odd." He stared at me, eyebrows pulled down in an effort to recall. "But it was today," he blurted out. "It was only today that I saw it."

"Talk sense, George," I said, laughing. "Tiggy must have died at least fifty years ago, and his cab is either in a museum or broken up for firewood."

But I could see that he was disturbed by what he had seen, or thought he had seen, outside the station, and later he brought up the subject again.

"You know that I'm not given to imagining things that aren't there," he began, as he sat in his deep leather arm-chair, with the flickering light of the fire animating the corners of the room. "And I admit that I was driving past the station and had only a glimpse. But there *was* a hansom cab there, *and* a horse with one white fetlock, *and*—and someone who struck me later as looking like Tiggy Smith." And he sat staring into the fire and stroking his moustache, a remnant of his Air Force days.

"George," I said briskly, to shake him out of his odd mood. "I have to deliver a manuscript to my agent in Tottenham Court Road tomorrow morning. Why not come with me, and we'll have a look for old Tiggy on the way back."

I tried to keep my voice light, as George was still staring into the fire, lost in thought.

We parked the car in Baron's Court Road and walked to the corner, where we could see across the road to the station.

There, by the kerb, stood a black hansom cab. And, in the shafts, a horse with one white fetlock.

High up on the box sat a figure wearing a grimy old bowler hat, and he had a horse blanket wrapped around his legs.

As we stood there staring, I felt a strange chill begin to ride up my spine, and I had, yes, a fear of going closer. To look up at the cabman's face, when I *knew* it would be Tiggy's face.

Tiggy, who had been an old, old man when I was a

10

young lad. It was impossible that he should be still alive.

The feeling of chill was making me shudder, and I started as George touched me on the arm.

"Brace up, Harry!" His voice was a dry whisper. "We must go and be certain. But it's ridiculous. Oh, come on, Harry."

He gripped my arm, as though somehow he didn't want to cross the road alone, even though it was in the full light of a bright September day.

We approached the cab from the back, and then we could hear the monotonous repetition of that old voice. "Keb sir, keb sir." We stopped alongside the high, red-lined wheel with its worn-down tyre.

" 'Ullo, young sirs." The tone of the voice changed. "Just 'ome from school? Goin' to ride with old Tiggy?"

I had the feeling that I was gripped in one of those dreams that terrify you, and you struggle to wake up, because you know that you're dreaming, but fear is holding you in the dream.

I forced myself to look up at the cabby. Slowly my eyes moved up the thin shabby figure, to the mittened hands, to the drawn dark face with its drooping moustache and bushy eyebrows under the brim of the old hat.

Yes, it was Tiggy's face that was staring down at me, and I stood cold and rigid, staring back at that thing from the past.

I tore my eyes away and looked at George. His face was white and set, and everything around us seemed to have gone grey and dim, as though the early afternoon had slid into the twilight of evening.

"It *is* Tiggy," he muttered. "And he called us young sirs, just as he used to."

" 'Oo else should it be?" came the voice from above us. " 'Op in, lads. It's Edith Road you live, if I remember right."

The slap back of the apron doors made the chill drain away from my body.

It all seemed so real. It *was* real. Real as it had been over half a century ago, when George and I had made

11

"Goin' to ride with old Tiggy?"

our naïve plans of how we were to set out into the world beyond school, and to conquer that world.

The cab springs creaked as we climbed in and settled back into the cushioned seat, and the smell of the leather closed us in as we watched the flicker of the reins above the cab roof.

Henry drew the cab away from the kerb, and his shoes clinked on the cobblestones as he trotted away down the hill.

Across Talgarth Road, once again narrow and quiet, and down towards Edith Road in the chill of the gathering darkness.

And then, as we sat swaying to the movement of the cab and watching the bobbing head of the horse in front of us, everything changed.

The cab seemed to melt away, the brightness of the day returned, and we were walking side by side along the pavement, by the wall of the school playing fields in Gliddon Road.

We stopped and stared at each other.

"Oh, this is madness!" burst out George, and he swung round, looking up and down the road, where there was no sign of the hansom cab that we'd been sitting in seconds before.

"Madness . . .? Hallucination . . .? Haunting . . .?" I muttered, the ideas chasing each other through my mind. "But George, it's happening to both of us. Two people can't have the same illusions at the same time. Or can they?"

"I don't know, Harry." He was becoming calmer now. "Tiggy spoke to us as though we were schoolboys still, and he's been dead for years. It looks as though we are only memories in the mind of his ghost."

"What rubbish!" I snapped at him. "Ghosts don't have memories."

"That's about all they do have, thank goodness," he answered me, as the traffic lights turned green and we crossed the main road back to the station.

There was no sign of the cab there, and I was still playing with the idea of hallucinations as we drove back to Chiswick.

13

"I say, Harry," said my brother as we sat in his study discussing the strange events of the afternoon. "It's not that I'm worried about being here on my own, but how about your staying here tonight? We could go and look for Tiggy Smith again in the morning. If my memory serves, we used to see him at the station as we went to school."

The following morning we found the cab waiting again, by the pillar box outside the Tube station.

It all seemed so real. The waiting cab, with Henry pawing at the road and twitching his ears. People were passing, but they took no notice of the old cab. Either they couldn't see it, or there was nothing there to see.

"This is crazy," I said. "If that is a ghost cab, why are we the only ones to see it? Has it got some special significance for us?"

"Don't ask me," said George in a mystified voice. "But I'm going to try something. Let's test old Tiggy."

He drew me forward with him, and we stood by the cab, which felt real and solid, the brass candle lamps by the side windows cleaned and polished.

"Good morning, Tiggy," said George in a firm voice. "We want to go to the Olympia. There's a stamp exhibition on there."

"Olympia, young sirs?" came the puzzled reply. "That don't seem right to me . . ." The voice of the old man grew fainter and fainter, and only half-heard mutterings came down to us.

I was staring at the cab, and that cold chill came over me again as I realised that it was getting vague and shadowy. That I could see right through it.

I could see through it to the other side of the road!

Then Tiggy's voice grew loud again, and the cab was once more solid and black.

"I must be getting old and forgetting things," he said with a short, uncertain laugh.

"Do you remember taking us home yesterday?" I asked him.

" 'Course I do, lad. Edith Road, number sixty-six.

You paid me a shillin' for the fare. Your black dog was barking at 'Enery 'ere. 'Op in lads, Olympia it is."

I glanced at George's face as we climbed into the cab. "You remember Carlo, our dog," I said. "He always barked at horses."

He nodded, and we settled back against the studded leather seat as Henry took us down to the crossroads.

We were both tense as we waited to see if the strange happenings of yesterday were to be repeated.

It came without warning.

The same dissolving of the cab around us into shadowy nothingness, and again we were on the pavement, at the same spot as before, with no sign of the cab in the empty street.

"Come on, Harry." George grabbed my arm. "We need help in sorting this out. Do you remember Gutsy Sheffield who was in the Fifth Form with me? Always eating sweets, aniseed balls mostly."

I frowned for a moment, thinking back.

"Yes, I remember him. Funny sort of chap. Never played football."

"That's him. I phoned him this morning. He's Sir John Sheffield now, the famous psychiatrist. I told him something of what's been happening to us. He said we're both mad, but he'll let us take him to lunch and talk about it."

Osmond's restaurant in Wigmore Street is one of those places where changes take place very slowly.

It is a place for leisurely lunches, where the table-cloths are smooth and white, the silverware old and battered, and the comfortable, high-backed chairs are upholstered in dark green plush.

Fathers introduce their sons to the place at an appropriate age, and they in turn pass on the introduction.

We had an excellent lunch there with our guest, a tubby little man with pink cheeks and piercing blue eyes, who listened with scarcely a question to our tale of impossible happenings, as he faced us across the table.

When we'd finished telling our story, he sat for a

minute or two in silence, elbow on table, with one plump cheek supported on his hand.

His eyes flickered from George's face to mine and back again several times, and then he gave a sort of quizzical grunt.

"Hmph," I suppose it's spelt. "I remember old Tiggy and his cab." And then he began to ask all sorts of odd questions.

Did we pass Baron's Court station frequently? Or our childhood home in Edith Road? Were our school years happy ones? Had there been any special event that tied in with Tiggy Smith?

He seemed especially interested in the transition when the cab melted away and we found ourselves on the pavement, and he went into fine details.

"Did you have any feeling of nausea?" he asked, as he fiddled about with the salt cellar. "Any sense of passing from one state to the other? You see, I'm working on the idea that you may have been walking all the time, and the cab and riding in it were something conjured up from your latent memories of places that had once been very familiar."

"But we've passed that way dozens of times over the years," I protested. "And now this thing has happened on two consecutive days. It's not only the riding in the cab, but we also spoke to Tiggy—and, and everything."

I stopped, rather lamely.

The psychiatrist said "Hmph" again, but in a somewhat different tone. Then he said that he'd think about the matter and phone George in the morning.

"I suppose that means that he doesn't know what it's all about," I said to George as we walked back to my car. "He'll go back and read up any similar cases he can find, and then cook up some sort of plausible explanation."

"If there is any sort of plausible explanation," he answered despondently.

I dropped him off at the Air Force Club in Piccadilly

and, as he was about to close the door, I reminded him of a suggestion that he'd made.

"You didn't mention to Gutsy," I said with a grin, "your idea of just being a memory in the mind of a ghost."

He smiled, rather wryly.

"No, I thought it better to leave that idea out of the conversation."

I drove back through the Park towards Baron's Court, for I was determined to see if the cab was there again.

It was there all right, just as though it was waiting for me.

As I crossed the road towards it I felt the chill again, and the brown shadowiness began to gather.

In the station entrance knelt a red-coated bootblack, with his Cherry Blossom foot-box and his brushes laid neatly beside it.

This, too, was something out of the past. There had been no bootblack there for many years.

I approached the kneeling man.

"Unusual thing to see today," I began. "A hansom cab, I mean. I thought it was all taxis now."

He looked up at me and jerked his head towards the roadside.

"What son, d'you mean old Tiggy? Blimey, e's been 'ere every day for years. 'Bout time 'e retired on 'is income." And he grinned widely.

Then an idea struck me.

Were these strange events some sort of time shift? A sort of distortion of the Fourth Dimension that one used to hear about so often?

First Tiggy and his cab, and now the bootblack.

Time distortion or ghostly visitation. I felt muzzy-headed and confused.

I went across to the cab and made myself look up at the driver.

"Tiggy," I said as calmly as I could. "Did you drive my brother and me home yesterday?"

He gave a deep sigh.

"Yus, I did, son. And I charged you a shillin'. You

17

two was my very last fare ever, and it ain't right to take money from your last fare. It's against the Rules. I knew you'd be by if I waited, but I don't know if it's against Standing Orders to return yer money. I'd better find out about 'ow I'd stand."

He unwrapped the blanket from around his legs and began to climb down from his high seat.

For some reason I stepped well back. I dreaded the test of physical contact.

"Won't be a minute, lad," he said, his moustache bristling as he spoke. "Must check with Orders, or it could be the Guardhouse."

He reached under the back of the cab, brought out a leather-bound nosebag and hitched the long strap over the horse's head.

" 'Ere, 'Enery, 'ave a feed while I'm gone," he muttered to the dismal-looking animal, and shuffled away towards the corner by the station.

It was all so real, so—so solid, that I had to insist to myself that it couldn't be happening. That Tiggy had died half a century ago.

I hurried after him as he crossed the side road, shuffling along, shoulders bent, and moving slowly in the gathering gloom.

It seemed an effort for his old legs to lift him up the far kerb, and he paused for a few moments, as though to gather his strength. Then on he went, his old bowler hat bobbing up and down with his slow steps.

He stopped again for a while, leaning on the brick wall of the cemetery, then he turned in through the gateway.

When I reached the entrance, I could see him ahead of me. He had left the gravelled roadway and started out along a well-worn path across the grass between the graves.

I knew that path well. It led to a gate on the far side of the cemetery that led out into Field Road.

It was the way George and I went—used to go— on our way to school in Greyhound Road.

Old Tiggy had stopped. He was leaning with both

arms on a headstone, panting heavily, his head hanging down.

My first impulse was to hurry forward and see if he was all right. But I stayed where I was, watching him, my head buzzing and whirling with the madness of my thoughts.

"My God, Harry," I muttered to myself. "He's a ghost or an illusion, or—or something. What if you can't touch him? What if your hands pass right through him?"

My whole body was gripped in an icy chill, and I could feel myself sweating cold. I knew that I couldn't go on, or go back, until the figure ahead of me moved first.

And if it turned back towards me—what would I do?

I thought of it coming closer and closer, reaching out for me. Trying to hold me and take me with it.

I tried to calm my nerves, tell myself that it was all a dream. Yes, that was it. I was having a nightmare. The whole thing was just a horrid nightmare.

It was something George had said about seeing a hansom cab. How long ago? Last night? Yes, last night.

I tried to wake myself up, but I was gripped tight in my fear. I struggled against it, and realised—this was no dream.

It was happening, happening to me now.

An old man, dead at least fifty years, was leaning, panting heavily, on a headstone not twenty paces ahead of me.

Darkness, the darkness of the grave, was closing in on all sides—and I couldn't move.

Staring ahead, I could see that the figure of Tiggy Smith was moving again. Away from me, thank God, away from me. It was shuffling forward along the path.

I felt urged on to follow him, and somehow I was getting closer and closer until, when he suddenly stopped by a grave close to the grey stone wall of the little chapel, I was scarcely three steps behind him.

The turmoil in my mind had sunk to a slow swirl of waiting for the thing to end. One way or another, I felt so tired that I couldn't care any more.

He was standing and staring at the grave, overgrown and neglected, the headstone dirty and blotched with green and yellow lichen, the wording, below a carved representation of a carriage wheel, scarcely visible.

"In memory of Tigham Smith, who departed this life 21st September 1923, aged 81 years."

The old man, standing by his own grave, began to turn towards me, and horror came screaming out of the darkness from all directions.

Under the old battered hat was no face! Only a white, gleaming skull, the jaws working in vain, as though it would speak.

I turned and fled on the wings of terror, my feet thumping on the hard-packed ground of the path.

A something behind me was calling, calling me back. Reaching out, slowing me.

Ahead was the cemetery gate, and beyond it was brightness.

My heart pounding in my chest, I fled through the gateway and out into the sunlight.

I stopped at the corner by the station, leaning back against the cool stone, sweating cold and panting, and watched as my heart slowed and steadied.

There was no sign of Tiggy's cab, and parked in the turning opposite I could see the bonnet of my car, the sunlight glinting from the polished chrome of the bumper in a single bar of brilliance.

It assured me of being in the world of today.

Still half shuddering, I forced myself to look back at the cemetery.

A young woman, pushing a pram, was passing the gate without even glancing inside. There was nothing unusual to attract her attention.

There was no need for me to go and assure myself that the skeleton shape of Tiggy Smith was no longer there.

I drove to George's place with a dull feeling in my mind. I didn't want to think about the happenings in the cemetery. I didn't want to think at all until I was with someone.

George was at home in his study, and, to my surprise, he had Sir John Sheffield there with him.

"Your case interests me," said the psychiatrist, blinking up at me. "So I've come over to look into it while the details are still fresh in your minds."

I shuddered.

"Fresh enough," I replied. And I related the ghastly experiences of the afternoon.

"Hmph," grunted Gutsy. "I'd like to see this ghost of yours. Could we go and see if Tiggy's back on station."

His laugh at his unintentional pun did nothing to ease the tension in my mind that my account of the events in the cemetery had built up.

From the corner opposite the station we could see the old cab by the kerb, and hear the drone of Tiggy's voice.

"Keb sir, keb sir, keb sir."

I glanced at George, who looked back and nodded.

Then we both looked at our companion.

"Yes," he began slowly. "It's just as I remember it from the old days. But the question is, why has he returned now, after fifty years?"

"That's what we want you to explain," said George. "And if it's just hallucination, why can *you* see it as well?"

"Oh, it's not hallucination. There's reason for his appearing. Father Riccardo might agree that he's to be released from limbo, but that he must purify himself first, and pay all his dues. And it seems that he has to pay back the last fare that he collected."

George snorted.

"Come off it, John. He's been dead for half a century. Don't tell me that he's come back again just to pay back an overcharge. Fifty years have gone by."

"But have they gone by for Tiggy? Or is it only yesterday for him? We don't really understand the true meaning of death. Does Tiggy understand that he died all those years ago? I'm going across to ask him."

We stared at him, but he had already started off across the road.

Slowly we followed, keeping well behind, uneasy as to what would happen.

Everything seemed so normal. The long sun-shadows of early evening. The noises of traffic and the sounds of footsteps and voices.

A sparrow hopped about in the gutter, pecking at the specks of feed that had blown into the kerb from when the horse had been feeding.

Then Sir John Sheffield was standing by the cab, looking up at Tiggy Smith.

"What's the date, Tiggy?" we heard him ask.

The old man stared down at him.

"Twenty-first, son," he answered in his deep voice. "September."

"What year, Tiggy?" And we waited for the reply.

"Now I don't want none of your lip, sonny. You know what year it is."

But Gutsy Sheffield stood his ground.

"Do you know it's nineteen twenty-three, Tiggy?"

"Course I know, I know what year it is."

The cabby's eyes strayed past his questioner and looked at George and me. His face brightened up.

"Ah, there you are, young sir. I've checked with Orders, and I got to give you back your fare. And if this boy goes to the same school as you do, he's learned plenty of sauce."

His hand came up, and a shiny coin came spinning towards us, glinting in the sunlight.

I caught it and it was icy cold.

The psychiatrist was still talking up at the old man.

"Do you know that it's nineteen seventy-three, and that you've been dead for fifty years?"

We waited.

22

It was as though the world had stopped, and there was no more movement.

But the cab and its driver were getting shadowy and faint, fading away.

And it was no longer there.

I seemed to hear the voice of Tiggy, as though it was hanging in the air.

"Course I know, I know what year it is."

We spoke very little on the way back to George's flat, except that Gutsy Sheffield said "extraordinary" several times.

Then, half lost in one of George's deep armchairs, he began to unburden his mind.

"Perhaps Father Riccardo would be right," he began. "Did you hear Tiggy answer anything to my last question?"

"Did *you*?" I countered.

"I'm not certain," he replied. "But I'm not sure if he was answering my last question, or whether it was an echo of his reply to the question before. Anyway, now that he's carried out the Rules, I don't suppose that we'll ever see Tiggy Smith again—or his cab." He paused and looked squarely at us. "That is, if we saw them at all."

But, even as he spoke, his eyes began to follow the movements of a bright new shilling that I was twisting between my fingers.

A bright new shilling bearing the head of King George V.

HOUSE OF GLASS

by CATHERINE GLEASON

KEVIN BROWN and his sister Millie climbed out of the taxi and sighed in unison as they surveyed the frontage of number 68, Hollydene Avenue. It was a tall, Victorian, terraced house in a large north-eastern town.

"Doesn't look much of a place to spend a holiday," grumbled Millie, as their mother paid the taxi-driver.

"It might be fun inside," said Kevin, without much conviction.

"Come on, you two. It's only for a week," said Mrs. Brown encouragingly. "I'll be picking you up next Saturday."

"A whole week," Millie said dismally, as she lugged her case to the doorstep.

"Now then," said her mother quite sharply. "Northumberland's very interesting and historical. There's Hadrian's Wall, and . . . all sorts of Roman places and things," she finished vaguely. "You'll be able to write essays about them when you go back to school."

"Whoopee," murmured Kevin, and Millie giggled. Unfortunately, Mrs. Brown heard.

"You must remember we're lucky to have a holiday at all this summer, with Daddy working away so much," she said, ringing the doorbell. "It's very good of Aunt Natalie to put you up, or rather put up with you, until we can go and join Daddy in Scotland."

"I bet Aunt Natalie is about seventy and smells of lavender," whispered Millie.

The door was opened by Aunt Natalie herself. She was about seventy and smelled of lavender.

"Welcome! Janet, my dear!" cried the old lady, embracing their mother. "And the dear children. Come inside, please." Her voice carried strong traces of her

24

original Russian tongue. She led them into the old-fashioned drawing-room, a slim, fragile little person with lively blue eyes and snowy hair piled into a neat chignon.

"It will be so good to have children in the house for a while—but I suppose I must not call you 'children', having grown so tall!"

"Well, Kevin's nearly thirteen and Millicent's eleven now, Natalie," said Mrs. Brown, laughing, "so they—is anything wrong?"

Aunt Natalie had stopped short and was gazing earnestly at Millie.

"No . . . that is . . . Janet, who does Millicent most resemble?"

"Ah, I thought you'd notice that," said Mrs. Brown. "She's very like Helena, isn't she?"

"To the life," said Aunt Natalie. Tears dimmed her eyes and there was a look of mingled pleasure and sorrow on her lined face.

The door opened and a plump, bustling woman came in. She was introduced to Millie and Kevin simply as Anna, Natalie Veronik's companion. Anna had also been born in Russia, but thirty years of living in England had muted her accent so that it was barely noticeable. She was good-natured and friendly, and about twenty years younger than their aunt, who explained that Anna would be taking them out in the car to the seaside and places of interest during their stay. Millie and Kevin felt much brighter as they followed her upstairs to their rooms on the second floor to unpack.

"Perhaps it's not going to be as dull here as we thought," said Kevin, and Millie agreed.

After a cheerful dinner, Mrs. Brown had to leave to catch the train home.

"Mummy," whispered Millie as they kissed her good-bye, "who's Helena?"

"Sssh." Their mother waved to Aunt Natalie and Anna, and led them out of earshot towards the taxi. "Helena Veronik was your aunt's daughter. She died young, and very tragically. You look very like her, Millie. Now, behave yourselves, both of you, and have a lovely

25

holiday. Anna's really a lot of fun and she'll look after you very well. Oh, and Millie, try not to mention your ballet lessons. Helena was a dancer, you see."

Mrs. Brown climbed into the taxi and waved as it whisked her away. Back inside the house, Millie and Kevin had a conference with Aunt Natalie and Anna. They decided on a trip to the country with a picnic lunch if the weather held the following day, to see the Wall and the site of a Roman camp which was being excavated. Before long they were yawning, tired out from their long journey, and Aunt Natalie suggested bed, which sounded a very good idea.

In his room, Kevin was annoyed to find his watch broken. He had left it on the bedside table after having a wash before dinner, and the glass had cracked across its face. He was wondering whether he had knocked or dropped it during the journey, when there was a knock at his door.

"Look at this mess, Kevin." Millie dumped her small vanity case on his bed. The mirror inside its lid had shattered, and slivers of glass glittered among the contents of the case.

"You must have bashed it on the train," said Kevin, helping her to take the pieces of glass out. "Hey, you've brought your ballet shoes along. I thought your teacher said you weren't to practise on your own at this stage?"

"Oh, a few *pliés* won't do any harm," said Millie, frowning as she picked bits of glass out of the case. "Mind your fingers, these pieces are very sharp. There, that's the lot. Thanks, Kevin. D'you think it's going to rain tomorrow?"

Kevin drew back his curtains and they peered anxiously out. The moon was riding serenely high in the clear night sky. Kevin turned to Millie with a grin.

"Not a chance," he said.

Sure enough, the next day dawned bright and beautiful. Aunt Natalie fussed happily over the picnic basket as they all piled into the car. They were all in a holiday mood as they headed for the country.

26

"Oh look!" cried Millie in astonishment as a sheep leapt from the grass verge and over a low hedge at their approach. "I didn't know sheep could jump!"

"Townie," teased Anna.

"They are quite agile, the sheep," their aunt told them.

Natalia Veronik was their mother's half-sister. Her father was a Russian who had moved with his family to Poland after the Russian Revolution. Natalie had married Serge Veronik, who had been killed, along with her mother, when the Nazis invaded Poland. She had managed to escape to England with her father and her little daughter Helena, and, of course, Anna. At first they settled in London, where her father had married again. He died shortly after Millie and Kevin's mother had been born, so the children had never known their grandfather. Natalie decided to live in Northumberland; she had never re-married.

All this the children gathered, in a rather sketchy way, from questioning their aunt as they drove along. She seemed quite pleased with their interest, and promised to tell them stories of her hair-raising escape from Poland through occupied Europe, thirty years ago.

They picnicked near the ancient Wall in the mild September sunshine. Probably because it was late in the year, there were no other tourists about, and the only thing that slightly marred their day was the return of Millie's hay fever, which had troubled her during the hot summer months. She tried not to make a fuss about it, but was secretly rather glad to be away from the fields and back in the car that evening.

There was no television at 68, Hollydene Avenue. While Aunt Natalie was resting in her room and Anna was cooking supper, Kevin yawned and said:

"I wonder what the attic rooms are like in this house? We haven't been up to the third floor yet."

"We can go and see if you—atishoo! 'Scuse me—like," said Millie.

They went out on to the landing, tiptoeing past their aunt's room so as not to wake her. There was no light bulb for the top floor, and the white attic door at the

27

top of the stairs gleamed pale and rather sinister through the evening gloom. For some reason he could not name, Kevin felt an odd reluctance to climb further.

"Achoo!" sneezed Millie behind him. "This wretched hay fever. Go on, Kevin."

Slowly he mounted another couple of steps.

"Millie! Kevin! What are you doing?" They froze in shock at their aunt's furious shout.

"Come down at once!"

Sheepishly, they turned back down the stairs. Their aunt was looking flushed, angry and somehow taller as they confronted her on the landing.

"We were just . . . just going to have a look at the attic, Aunt Natalie," stammered Millie.

"There is nothing of interest up there. You must avoid that part of the house, *especially after dark*."

Was it imagination, or was there a trace of fear in her voice?

"Come to supper now, I am sure it must be ready." She turned and stalked downstairs.

Kevin shrugged. "Well, that's it then. Probably just an old lumber room."

Millie nodded, but her curiosity was aroused.

Aunt Natalie was frosty over supper, for which they had a delicious kind of Russian stew called goulash. She thawed over their game of Scrabble later, however, and things were back to normal by the time they went to bed.

Anna took them to a stables for an early ride the next morning. As they trotted down a woodland lane, Millie told Kevin of the peculiarly vivid dream she'd had during the night.

"There was a ballerina," she said. "I couldn't see her face, but she danced beautifully, and she kept beckoning for me to follow her. I must have sleep-walked, because I woke up standing in the middle of the room. I'd stubbed my toe on the wardrobe, you see, and that's what wakened me."

Kevin laughed. "You think about nothing but dancing these days. When you're a professional you'll have to

28

change your name, you know—how about Millicenta Brownovich?"

"Sarcastic—achoo!—clot!" yelled Millie in mock rage as her brother cantered on down the path.

When they came back to Hollydene Avenue, Aunt Natalie was getting ready to go shopping with Anna.

"Are you sure you two won't come along?" she asked.

"No thanks, Aunt," said Kevin, repressing a shudder. Looking at ladies' hats was not his idea of fun.

When they had gone, Millie slipped out to the corner shop for a large bottle of lemonade. She left it on the coffee-table in the living room and went into the kitchen, where Kevin was piling biscuits on to a plate.

"Can you see any glasses anywhere?" she asked.

"There they are," said Kevin, reaching for a couple of Pyrex ones on a shelf. Suddenly there was a splintering crash from the next room. They rushed in to find the bottle in pieces on the floor, and lemonade soaking into the rug.

"You clumsy idiot, Millie! You must have left it on the edge!"

"I did not!" shouted Millie. "I put it right in the middle of the table. It must have fallen off by itself!"

"Oh, don't be so silly," said Kevin angrily. "It couldn't have!"

A row developed, and by lunchtime they were hardly speaking. Kevin had collected the broken glass and hidden it in the dustbin, and Millie managed to dry the rug fairly well in front of the fire.

They were meant to go to a football match that afternoon, but Millie's hay fever had worsened, so Anna took Kevin to the match and Millie sprawled sulking on a sofa, sneezing, with streaming eyes and a nagging headache. Aunt Natalie started a game of Monopoly with her, but nodded off after a few minutes. Millie fidgeted, bored, and tried to sneeze quietly. Then she had an idea. When she was sure her aunt was properly asleep, she crept noiselessly out of the room and up the stairs, towards the attic.

Kevin enjoyed his soccer. When they returned, he

29

lingered in the back garden for a few practice kicks on his own. He dribbled the football up and down the path for a few minutes, then aimed a kick at the wall. Unfortunately the ball went wide and travelled straight for the kitchen window. Kevin closed his eyes and clapped his hands over his ears against the expected crash. The ball hit the window with a loud thud and bounced back harmlessly, the window intact. Kevin was astonished. Suddenly a disturbing thought struck him. He walked up to the kitchen window and began to examine it closely.

"Anna," said Aunt Natalie worriedly, "I found the children going up to explore the attic yesterday."

"Oh no!" gasped Anna. "Did they see inside?"

The old lady shook her head. "I stopped them on the stairs."

"Thank goodness for that." Anna sank into a chair. "What did you say to them?"

"Simply that there is nothing to interest them. That they must not go to the third storey."

"But Natalia, hadn't we better tell them about the attic? Warn them?"

"No, Anna, I don't think so," she replied. "Why disturb their peace of mind?"

"But they may be curious," argued Anna, "and attempt another visit."

Natalia Veronik sighed wearily. "I think not," she said. "There is plenty to occupy them here, and there is no danger during the hours of daylight." Her lip trembled, and she turned away abruptly.

"My poor Helena . . ."

Millie and Kevin met up before supper that evening. Both were bursting to tell what they had found out that afternoon, but the morning's quarrel had left them standing on their dignity.

It was Kevin who spoke first.

"How's your hay fever?" he asked grudgingly.

"Much better, thanks."

There was a pause, then they both said together:

"I've got something to tell you!"

"You first," said Kevin with a grin.

"Well, I went up to the attic this afternoon when Aunt Natalie was asleep, and what do you think?—It's a ballet studio! It must have been Helena's. The floor's wooden, there's a practice bar, and one wall's covered by a huge mirror with a kind of house carved into the glass. It looks like a castle in a fairy tale. There are dozens of books about ballet, some cups and awards, and . . . a wheelchair."

"A wheelchair?"

"Yes. I suppose Helena must have had an accident or something. But, Kevin, it's a perfect place to practise. It's just like Mrs. Carson's ballet school at home. I wonder why Aunt Natalie didn't tell us about it? Do you think she'd let me use it if I told her I'm learning to dance?"

Kevin shook his head. "Mum said not to mention it. Are you sure about the mirror in the attic? Because there's something queer about this house."

Millie looked bewildered. "How do you mean?" she asked.

"Well, nothing else here is made of glass."

"But there are mirrors, and windows . . ."

"Yes, but they're not ordinary glass. I can't be absolutely sure, of course, but I'm pretty certain that they're a kind of plastic substitute, or that special reinforced glass they use for car windscreens. All the drinking glasses are Pyrex, there are no glass ornaments, no television . . ."

"I see," said Millie slowly. "Whenever we've brought glass into the house—your watch, my mirror, that bottle this morning—they're smashed."

"Exactly," said Kevin excitedly. "We have to find out more about Helena Veronik, Millie, because I'm sure it all ties in with her——"

They were interrupted by Anna calling them down to supper.

Later in the evening, Aunt Natalie told them amazing stories of her escape to England. Millie and Kevin listened spellbound as she spoke of dangerous incidents, which sounded like television adventures to them, but which were

31

common enough in those desperate years. She talked on, her strangely-accented voice making the tales compelling and real. Her last story was of hiding with Anna in a hayrick, holding their breaths as the tramp of jackboots came nearer, louder . . . then the tremendous relief as the patrol passed by, and the footsteps faded.

"It's just as well we didn't suffer from hay fever, Millie," said Anna, smiling.

"Yes, indeed," chuckled their aunt. "One sneeze and we surely should have been discovered! Well, all this talking has made me tired, and I must go to bed. Goodnight, my dears." She kissed them and left the room.

Kevin turned immediately to Anna. "You and Aunt Natalie have certainly had very exciting lives," he began.

"Too exciting, perhaps, and very sad sometimes," she replied.

"Will you tell us about Helena, Anna?" asked Millie, moving her chair closer. "She would have been our cousin if she had lived, wouldn't she?"

Anna stared at them for a few moments, then seemed to make up her mind.

"Very well. Helena Veronik was a dancer," she began. "The attic room was converted into a studio for her, and she used to spend nearly all her free time there, practising, when she wasn't having lessons. She had a kind of house etched into a mirror up there, and she often used to say that she wished it were real, so that she could live there and dance and dance forever. Well, she was a very gifted dancer, and at sixteen she seemed all set for a brilliant career. Then she fell in love with a worthless man." Anna frowned at the memory. "One day she missed a class to go out driving with him in the country, and he drove too recklessly and crashed the car. He was unharmed, but Helena hurt her back and could no longer walk. Her fiancé deserted her, and so she lost everything."

"That's awful. What happened to her then?" Kevin prompted, as Anna paused.

"Helena used to spend hours in her wheelchair, just staring into the mirror. One day she died. It may have been the result of her spinal injury, or perhaps a broken

32

heart. To Natalia, of course, her daughter's memory is sacred, and that is why she does not wish anyone, ever, to visit the studio. That is all you need to know about Helena, my dears."

Anna stood up briskly. "Heavens, look at the time—bed, both of you!"

"Do you think Anna told us everything?" asked Millie, half an hour later. She had crept into her brother's room for a whispered conference as soon as the house was silent. "Because what she said doesn't really explain the broken glass, does it? Unless . . ." She shuddered. "Unless there's some sort of a spell on the glass in this house because of the mirror upstairs."

"Oh, it's probably just a coincidence." Kevin's attempted laugh sounded hollow.

"But, Kevin, what if Helena's still—I mean, if she's . . ."

"A ghost?" Kevin frowned. "No, that's impossible. Don't think about it. Even if the house *is* haunted, and I don't believe it is, it can't effect us as long as we don't go near the studio."

"I suppose not." Millie yawned. "Well, I'm going to bed now. Goodnight."

"Goodnight," said Kevin.

Both of them had quite forgotten Millie's dream of the previous evening.

Towards midnight, Kevin woke with a start, and the vague feeling that something was wrong. It was the same sense of unease that he had felt outside the attic door. He tried to ignore it, telling himself that he was imagining things.

Then, very distantly and sweetly, he heard music playing. Tchaikovsky, or some such . . .

Ballet music! In a second, Kevin was out of bed and padding to his sister's room. Millie's bed was empty. As quickly and quietly as he could, Kevin ran along the landing and up the stairs towards the attic. The white door was slightly open, and he could see a phosphorescent-like glow from inside.

Cautiously he pushed open the door and entered the

studio. The scene before him rooted him to the ground with amazement. The source of the strange light was the mirror, and the turreted house which was carved upon it seemed lit from within by an unearthly glow. Millie, dressed in her tunic and ballet shoes, was standing motionless, her back to him, one hand resting on the practice bar. She seemed to be staring, hypnotised, at the slender, fragile figure of a ballerina, who was dancing slowly before her to the strains of the faint music.

Time seemed to have run down, like a slow-motion film, and Kevin could not tell if the dancer was outside the mirror or the mirror had become three-dimensional. The ballerina was deathly white, and lustreless as chalk. She drifted and swayed with the lazy grace of sea-ferns, her eyes blank and dark and fixed upon his sister.

As he watched, the dancer glided over to Millie and took her hands, and, stepping backwards, pulled her gently towards the eerie light. What would happen when they reached the house of glass? Would they vanish inside for ever?

Panic-stricken, Kevin tried to shout, but his throat was tight with fear. Millie was moving like a sleep-walker, ever closer to the haunted mirror. Kevin glanced wildly round, and suddenly noticed a crystal trophy on a table near his hand. Without pausing to think, he picked it up and hurled it with all of his strength at the glass.

Instantly the glow faded, the music vanished and the mirror shattered silently, jagged fragments and splinters of glass scattering on to the floor soundlessly, as though they were autumn leaves. Then the studio was filled with the sound of a great peaceful sigh, and, dimly in the moonlight, the slight shade sped towards the open window and was gone.

Kevin ran to Millie, who was curled up on the floor, and shook her urgently. She opened her eyes and sat up, yawning and blinking.

" 'Morning," she mumbled drowsily. "I had *such* a funny dream." She gazed around vaguely, then stared at Kevin in astonishment. "What are we doing in here? Who broke the mirror?"

The ballerina was deathly white . . .

"Sssh! Let's get out."

They crept away from the studio, down to Kevin's room, where he told Millie all that had happened.

"It sounds as if I had a narrow escape," said Millie gravely, when he had finished. "I dreamed that Helena was taking me to a kind of fairyland. I didn't know it was all really happening. Why didn't Aunt Natalie warn us?"

"I suppose she thought we were safe enough as long as we didn't got into the studio at night," said Kevin. "She didn't know about your ballet lessons, so she couldn't reckon on Helena feeling a kind of bond with you, and wanting to take you with her into the world that imprisoned her, before the house of glass and the spell that bound her were broken."

Millie shivered. "I suppose we'll have to tell Aunt Natalie in the morning," she said.

"Yes, we will," answered Kevin thoughtfully.

"But I think she will be glad to know that Helena Veronik is free now, and resting peacefully at last."

THE MURDEROUS GHOSTS

by ROSEMARY TIMPERLEY

IT was his first Channel crossing. His first journey abroad, in fact. Abroad. Another world. And the sea had to be crossed before one got there. It was exciting. Strange, too. The rocking of the boat. Did he feel sea-sick? He'd been warned that he might. No, not sick exactly. Just dazed. A queer rhythm going on inside him, back and forth, back and forth. Or was it up and down, up and down? It was a weird, swooping mixture of the two. It made him feel different . . . unreal . . .

So he'd left his parents in the bar and come up on deck, even though all was grey and misty and there was a fleck of rain in the air. No one was about, at first.

He leaned on the rail and looked down into the water. Suddenly he thought of all that depth of sea beneath them. Suppose they sank! Nonsense. Channel steamers didn't sink——

"I hope she's sunk all right," said a voice behind him. A booming sort of voice, like a distant fog-horn.

Startled, he turned to see a tall man with a big black beard and moustache. "Seen my wife?" the man asked.

"Er—no—I haven't seen anyone," said Jack.

"Oh. Good. I expect she's sunk all right then. I was afraid she might have bobbed up, like a balloon." Blackbeard peered over the side, into the murky water. "No sign, thank goodness," he said. "Didn't really think there would be, but you never know with a persistent woman like Annabel."

"Annabel?" echoed Jack.

"My wife. Couldn't stand her any longer. Brought her on this boat for a trip to the other side. Pushed her overboard. Felt a bit sea-sick afterwards. Rested in the cabin.

Then I was suddenly scared in case she'd bobbed up. No. No sign of her. Whew!"

He brought out a large grey handkerchief and mopped his brow, nose, cheeks, beard, moustache and eyes, then he smiled at Jack.

"Never get married, young man," he said.

"I don't think I ever would," Jack responded seriously. "I don't care much for females. They seem unnatural, somehow."

"Unnatural. Never said a truer word," agreed Black-beard. "Their minds don't work, that's the trouble. They have feelings. All these emotions, perceptions, imaginings. Before I brought her on board, my wife said: 'You're going to try to get rid of me. I feel it in my bones.' Well, how could she know? Unnatural. But I did more than try. I *have* got rid of her. I hope." He looked over the side again. "Yes, she must have well and truly sunk by now. Fat woman. Do you know why wives are fat while girl friends are slim?"

Jack shook his head.

"Because wives relax, boy. They've got their man. They're secure for life. They have an income without work. Take Annabel. Beautiful girl when she was young. Loved her."

Tears suddenly filled his eyes and rolled down into his moustache and beard, so that his face in the greyness shone with mingled tears and rain. "Yes, loved her once. Really did!"

"Why?" asked Jack.

"Why? She was lively, affectionate, aimed to please. But once she had a ring on her finger and a house to sit in, she just sat. Sat and ate sweets and read novels and watched telly. She sat and grew fat and she always wore black. Said she was 'in mourning for her life'. That's a quote from some Russian play she'd seen on telly. She said I had no soul. Well, I *had* to get rid of her."

"A man's gotta do what a man's gotta do," said Jack, quoting a recent telly advert.

"Exactly," said Blackbeard, with a sigh.

Jack said, "You are pulling my leg, aren't you? I mean—you didn't really push her overboard."

"Of course I did," fog-horned the man. "What else are we talking about? I wanted to be free!"

"I like to be free, too," agreed Jack, "but I wouldn't drown anyone to be it. It's not right to kill people, even if they're a nuisance. Suppose she comes back and haunts you."

"Annabel, a ghost? Ever heard of a *fat* ghost? No . . ." And at that moment a huge blackness seemed to form itself out of the nothingness of the mist, and a woman's voice said: "Is that you, Gregory?"

Blackbeard jumped so much that he nearly went over the side.

"Annabel!" he gasped. "But you're dead!"

"So are you," said the fat woman in black. She had a sweet, delicate voice. "I poisoned your drink before you drowned me. You're lying dead in our cabin at this moment, only you're so insensitive you don't realise it." She turned to Jack. "Hello, little boy. Can you see us?"

Jack nodded.

"Really? Dear child, you must be psychic. Gregory, it'll be interesting for us to wander around and find out who sees us and who doesn't. We can separate the sensitives from the clodhoppers."

"How did you get out of the water?" demanded her husband.

"I didn't. That is, my body didn't. But *I'm* here. You really are dead, Gregory, otherwise you wouldn't be able to see me. *You're* not psychic. You have no more spirituality than a pudding. If you don't believe me, go along to the cabin and see for yourself."

"I did lie down in the cabin, feeling sick, after I'd drowned you," the man admitted. "It was a shock to my system. I remembered some of the old, happy times, before the rot set in. Then I pulled myself together and came up here."

"You pulled yourself together and came out of your

body, dear, just as I did," said his wife. "Go down to the cabin and take a look at your old self."

"Oh, all right—just to prove you wrong." Blackbeard vanished.

The woman turned to Jack. "Are Gregory and I the first ghosts you've ever met?'" she asked chattily.

"Guess so," muttered Jack—not that he believed for one minute that either of them was a ghost, but he thought it best to humour them. "What did you poison your husband with?" he asked, in the same chatty tone as the woman.

"Weed-killer," she answered with a chuckle. "Suitable, eh? He looks like an odd sort of weed, with all that hair. I knew he was going to drown me, you see. I'm a very sensitive creature and I felt it in my bones. It's because I always felt things so intensely in my bones that I let myself grow fat, to protect my bones. But I went on being sensitive. Anyway, I decided that if he could be so selfish and unfriendly as to murder me, I'd do the same to him. Tit for tat. Poor Gregory. Now he's lost his own life but he hasn't lost me. We'll be bound together for all eternity, the couple who murdered each other. What closer tie? But I will try to be nicer to him now. What do you think of it all?"

"You won't like it if I tell you what I honestly think," said Jack.

"Never mind, child. Out with it."

"I think," Jack said carefully, "that the rocking of the boat and maybe quite a lot of duty-free wallop at the bar has made you and your husband have delusions. You're having a sort of shared D.T.'s. That," he explained patiently, "is *delirium tremens*. Alcoholics have it. They see things that aren't there, like green snakes and pink elephants and whatnot, and have other peculiar experiences. You may have wanted to do each other in, but you obviously didn't or you wouldn't be here. That's what I think."

He also thought she might be angered. Grown-ups usually resent very much being told that they're drunk, especially by a child, but she smiled at him affectionately.

"You dear little soul," she said. "Here you are, psychic as they make 'em, communing with ghosts, and you don't even realise it. I expect a lot of people you've talked to during your life have been ghosts, and you simply haven't known. You must take notice next time you bump into someone and feel nothing—or shake hands with someone, and find yourself grasping thin air."

She sighed, and a cool wind blew. "Do you know what I'm going to miss most now I'm a ghost?"

"The telly?"

"Oh, no. I can still watch that. I'll be invisible to most people, so I can walk into any living-room and join the family. Maybe the dog will growl or the cat's fur will stand on end or the room will turn chilly, but no one will know it's me. No, what I shall miss is eating. I've really enjoyed eating, since I was married and could let my looks go. Gregory likes his grub, too. He'll miss eating. We'll have that in common. A shared loss."

"But it'll be convenient," said Jack, joining in her "game" again instead of being sceptical. "If you don't need food, you won't need money. Everything will be free."

"That's true. We shall be able to travel the world without needing any food to sustain us, and without paying any fares. Yes, it'll be lovely. We'll travel for the rest of our lives."

"Lives? If you're both dead?" said Jack sharply.

"Don't you try to catch me out, young man. The after-life is as much a life as the one you've got. I don't know everything about it yet as I'm still a 'new girl', but I'm finding my way around."

Blackbeard appeared suddenly. He grinned. "Our cabin is empty," he said. "No body."

"That's nothing," said Annabel. "It only means that the steward found it while we were talking here and had you put wherever they do put dead bodies on board ship."

"Where would that be?" Jack asked, fascinated.

"I don't know," she said. "Gregory and I can go invisible walk-about later and find what they've done with him. In the old slave ships they used to put dead slaves

41

in the cooking-pot to feed the crew. Perhaps the Captain will be having a fry-up of Gregory's kidneys for breakfast. I'd quite fancy that myself, with some bacon and a tomato —and butter and marmalade and toast——"

"Trust you to think of nothing but your stomach, even when you're dead!" blazed Gregory, then made a super-human effort to control his irritation. "Annabel, please understand that you *are* dead now—dead as mutton— dead as a door-nail—dead as the dodo——"

"Perhaps we'll meet a dodo on our travels," his wife said dreamily.

"—and therefore," Blackbeard continued, "you have no right to be here. It's not suitable. Dead people are supposed to lie down——"

"But you didn't, Gregory, and we're in the same boat. Where shall we go then?" She looked at Jack. "Any suggestions?"

"I suggest," said Jack, deciding at this moment that whatever work he took up in life he would not be a mental nurse or warden of a home for alcoholics, "that you go to the bar and have a cup of strong black coffee together— and make friends."

"Isn't he sweet?" said Annabel. "He still doesn't believe that we're ghosts."

"You've had a jolly good fight," said Jack, "drowning and poisoning each other, or pretending to, and now it's time to make up and be friends. Please! It would be—well —nice," he concluded feebly.

Husband and wife regarded each other.

"He's right," said Annabel. "It would be nice. We'll be together for ever now, Gregory, so let's be friends. I apologise for poisoning you with weed-killer."

"Now you apologise to her for whatever you did," said Jack.

"I apologise for drowning you," muttered Blackbeard. "I *was* sorry afterwards, actually."

"Now shake hands," said Jack.

They did, and Annabel said: "Place your hand on ours, to give us your blessing."

42

Jack tried to do so, but the boat lurched at that moment so he didn't actually touch the clasped hands.

"Oh, I do feel peculiar," said Blackbeard, in the tone of a bewildered fog-horn.

"So do I, love, but we'll soon get accustomed," said Annabel.

"I feel a bit sick, too. Excuse me," said Jack, and left them standing together at the rail. Cor! he thought. A right couple of loonies. But interesting. Leaves you with something to think about.

He walked on another part of the deck until his sickish feeling wore off, then began to make his way to the bar to rejoin his parents. As he passed a door marked MEDICAL ROOM, a man with a stethoscope round his neck—apparently a doctor—was just coming out and saying to another man: "It wasn't ordinary sea-sickness. People don't die of that, although they often feel as if they're dying. Food-poisoning, more like." And just for a second Jack wondered if Annabel's tale of poisoning was true, and those two had been ghosts, and he really was psychic. He tried bumping into a few people to see if he felt anything. He felt the bumps all right. So did his victims—"Look where you're going, lad! My corns are not for stamping on!"

At last he reached his parents at their table in the bar.

"Feeling seedy, darling? You're very pale," said his mother. "It is rather a rough crossing."

"You can say that again," said Jack.

His father brought him a glass of lemonade and he sat there sipping it. Everything settled back into a kind of normality. He even wondered if he'd dreamed those two people on deck. All this rocking and swaying did make one light-headed. Perhaps he'd imagined the whole incident——

Then the door of the bar swung open and the mysterious couple, Blackbeard and his wife, walked in, large as life and arm-in-arm. They didn't look at all drunk—and they'd made friends. Jack felt he'd had some share in that and, when they smiled and waved at him, he smiled and waved back. They went to sit at a table some distance away, but didn't order anything.

"Who were you waving to?" asked his mother.

"The couple that's just sat down over there. I met them on deck. They'd had a bit of a tiff but they're O.K. now."

He returned his empty lemonade glass to the counter and, as he did so, heard one of the assistants say to the other: "Rough old crossing in more senses than one. A Mr. Gregory Lake has died of food-poisoning, and his wife is missing, presumed drowned."

Can't be the same as my couple, thought Jack, giving another wave and smile to his friends. But they were absorbed in each other now, holding hands across the table—and she seemed to be slimmer than before, and prettier—and he looked younger and his beard was less aggressive——

His mother asked: "Jack, who do you keep waving to?"

"That couple—I told you—at that table." He pointed.

"But that table," said his mother, "is empty."

Jack went cold and whispered: "Are you sure?"

"Of course I'm sure. What's the matter with you?"

"I'm psychic," said Jack, with wonder and a touch of pride.

"Sea-sick, more like," said his father. "Never mind, Jack, boy. We'll soon be on the other side. It's like another world over there."

True enough, the ship was approaching the shore and the mist had cleared. They came out of it as if it had been a dream. They went to the rail to watch the land approach.

And suddenly Jack saw two figures who were going to reach the other side before the ship made port. They were walking, or floating, rather, ahead of the ship. They looked absurd, yet touching at the same time, the rather plump woman in black and the tall bearded man, hand-in-hand, skimming across the water . . .

They're in love again, Jack thought proudly, and I "brought them together". But he was congratulating himself a bit too soon for, as he watched, the outline of the two figures became rather less lovey-dovey. Annabel looked as if she'd given Gregory a pretty sharp kick on the ankle—and he'd kicked her back. The two heads turned towards each other, in obvious argument.

What were they saying?

A seagull shrilled across the sky. Through its cry, Jack heard Annabel's voice: "I am being nice—nice—nice—nice——"; and through the noise of a distant fog-horn came Gregory's angry: "Oh, you—you—you—you—YOU!"

THE HAUNTED CIRCUS

by SYDNEY J. BOUNDS

DIANNE lost her balance and fell to the padded mat—
again.

"Are you hurt, dear?" her mother asked anxiously.

"Of course she isn't hurt," her father said testily. "Now,
Dianne, you must try again, and keep trying. It's practice
that counts in our business."

Dianne sighed as she climbed the steps to the small
platform leading to the wire stretched across the circus
ring. It was only six feet above the ground, and how to
fall was the first thing she had been taught.

Being the daughter of a pair of circus acrobats was
sometimes a hard thing to live up to. "Dianne on the
Silver Wire" . . . some hope! She wasn't very good, and
she knew it. The height didn't worry her, or falling; it was
being laughed at she couldn't stand. Imagine, the daughter
of acrobats who couldn't even balance on a wire! And
not just any old acrobats. Her father and mother were the
Red Devils, the star attraction of Ringwall's circus.

Her father turned away. "There's something new I want
to try."

Dianne watched her parents climb a swaying ladder
to the high trapeze. Forgotten already . . . the story of
my life, she thought sadly.

She wandered slowly across the ring, a thin figure in
patched tights, and made for the menagerie. Since Charley
had died, the only real friends she had were the animals.
Charley the Clown had always found time to talk to her,
even though circus people were constantly busy. Dianne,
at fourteen, had never known loneliness before.

Maxine, the bareback rider, was brushing her horse
for the evening show and Dianne helped her. Besides the
horses, the circus had a lion act, and performing dogs.

"I wish I could work with animals all the time," Dianne said wistfully.

Maxine smiled. "I don't think your parents would like that."

"I suppose not."

When the horses were groomed, Dianne returned to the Big Top. She climbed the steps and started across the wire. Practice, practice, practice, she thought. She was half way across when she realised there was someone beside her, and froze. There couldn't be, not six feet off the ground.

She balanced carefully, watching the figure from the corner of her eye. It looked like Charley, in his spangled clown's costume, his face whitened for the ring. The figure floated in the air beside the wire.

A voice whispered, "Come on, Di, I know you can do it. Do it for Charley."

She knew that voice; no one else called her "Di", ever . . .

Suddenly frightened, she jumped down to the mat.

Carl, the lion-tamer, was passing and saw her pale face. He stopped. "Are you all right, Dianne?"

She glanced up at the wire, but there was no one there now. "Did you see anybody? Or hear anything?"

"No." Carl was mystified. "What is it?"

"Oh, nothing."

Dianne hurried away. Charley had come back; no, that wasn't right. His ghost had come back. She didn't have to be frightened, Charley wouldn't hurt her—but it was still a shock, even if he only whispered encouragement.

Outside the Big Top, a queue was forming, and soon she was caught up in the preparations for the show. Ring-wall's circus was a small one, which meant that the performers doubled up; everyone had two, or even three jobs to do. Every piece of equipment had to be in its exact place, and it was Dianne's job to retrieve small items as they were no longer needed.

The seats were filling, the band played "The Entry of the Gladiators", and the clowns ran into the ring.

Dianne was with Maxine, helping to hold the horses.

She had quite recovered now and was beginning to think she had only imagined that she'd seen Charley when she heard his voice at her side.

"Don't worry, Di, you'll do it one day."

She turned, startled, but there was nobody there.

The horses snorted and broke free, galloping into the ring and running wild. The clowns scrambled over the barrier to join the audience, and it took Maxine a long time to get them under control again. Her act was ruined.

"I don't know what got into them," she fretted. "It was just as if something spooked them."

Tom Ringwall, the circus owner, looked worried. "We can't afford to let that happen again," he said. "It's the sort of thing that could ruin our reputation."

Dianne thought she could have told them what had frightened the horses, but decided to say nothing. She knew the circus was moving to another town when the performance ended and she didn't think Charley's ghost would be following them.

But in that she was wrong . . .

When the Big Top was erected in Wexley, Dianne started to practise her wire-walk. Charley's ghost bobbed along beside her, making encouraging remarks.

"There's nothing to worry about, Di. Keep at it."

Dianne overbalanced and fell. She was more frightened than she wanted to admit; suppose the ghost never stopped haunting her?

"Oh, leave me alone!" she burst out hysterically.

Her mother overheard and looked startled. "What was that, dear? Is someone bothering you?"

Dianne shook her head and ran away. No one else saw the ghostly clown, so who would believe her?

As the time drew near for the evening performance, the lions became restless. They prowled up and down their cage, roaring, their tails lashing angrily.

Tom Ringwall hurried up to see what was wrong.

Carl stared gloomily at his cats through the bars of the cage.

"They can't perform like this, Mr. Ringwall. It would be too dangerous. Something's upset them."

The circus owner looked unhappy. "The audience is going to feel cheated if they don't see a lion act—but I have to agree, we can't send them into the ring in this state."

The news that the lions would not be appearing spread fast—and attendance dropped. Tom Ringwall was worried.

"This is a disaster! The circus may have to close if we have any more trouble with the animals."

Only Dianne knew what was wrong. The animals were sensitive; they knew a ghost was around and didn't like it.

The show went on as usual, to a small audience. Dianne was retrieving some props from the ring when Charley whispered in her ear:

"It'll soon be your turn, Di. Just keep trying."

She looked round, startled, and hissed: "You've got to leave me alone, Charley. I'll be all right. You're frightening the animals and spoiling the show."

She didn't know whether he heard her or not, and wondered if she should stop practising altogether. Would the dead clown stop haunting her then?

Next morning, before practice, she tried to tell her father. He looked stern and cut in before she could explain properly.

"No, Dianne, you can't give up—that wouldn't be professional. You know we want you to train for our trapeze act as soon as you've mastered the wire. It's only a question of time, so keep practising."

Dianne sighed, climbed the steps to her wire and started to walk. Below, in another part of the ring, Maxine was putting her performing dogs through a new routine.

Dianne was halfway across when Charley appeared beside her, whispering encouragement.

"That's it, Di. Try, try, try again . . ."

Dianne paused, balancing carefully. She looked down to see if Maxine had seen or heard anything. Obviously not. But her dogs had. Scenting the ghost, they howled and ran with their tails between their legs.

Tom Ringwall stared in dismay. "What the deuce is

Charley appeared beside her . . .

going on? All our animal acts seem to have a jinx on them."

Maxine was close to tears. "I don't understand it, Mr. Ringwall. The dogs were doing so well—they were nearly ready to go into the ring."

Charley still floated in the air beside Dianne. No one else saw him and he, obviously, was unaware that the dogs had bolted.

Suddenly, Dianne started to listen intently to what he had to say. It seemed almost as if he could read her mind. And what Charley had to say made Dianne think furiously.

Is that how you exorcised the ghost of a clown? she wondered. She blamed herself for the failure of the circus and felt desperate enough to try anything.

She hurried back to her parents' caravan and sat down with pencil and paper to work out the idea Charley had given her. She'd need a wig, and a cane, and——

There was a knock at the door and Tom Ringwall's voice: "Dianne?"

"Yes, I'm here."

When she opened the door, the circus boss was looking very unhappy.

"It's the dogs," he said. "They're still misbehaving and will have to be left out of tonight's show. We need an act to fill ten minutes. Do you think you're ready to step in?"

Dianne gasped with pleasure; this was the chance she needed. "Oh yes, Mr. Ringwall—I'm sure I can manage it!"

"That's fine, then."

At the evening performance, it wasn't only the audience who got a surprise. The circus folk had assumed that Dianne would be doing the act she had practised for weeks.

Instead, she ran into the ring wearing the spangled costume of a clown, with her face whitened. And a trampoline had been placed under the wire. At first, Dianne hesitated on the platform, pretending to be afraid of the wire. She essayed a few steps like a complete beginner;

51

her cane caught in her wig and tore it off. Swaying wildly, she tried to get the wig off the cane, lost her balance and fell . . . she rebounded from the trampoline and swung like a monkey, one-handed, from the wire. Then she was up again and performing more of Charley's tricks she had adapted for use on the wire. She was so caught up in her new act that she was, at first, only distantly aware of people laughing. The audience and the other circus performers roared at her antics, and now she began to appreciate laughter as only a clown can. It gave her a warm feeling and she worked harder for more laughs.

Dancing in the air beside her, unseen by anyone else, the ghost of Charley the Clown laughed loudest of all. As her act came to a climax, he chuckled: "I knew you could do it, Di. Good luck . . ."

His voice faded away, lost in a barrage of applause.

Her parents were proud of her first-time success, and the animals behaved perfectly again. Sometimes, though, as she capered on the wire and the audience nearly died of laughing, Dianne felt a little sad inside, because she longed to see Charley's ghost bobbing along beside her. But she knew, now, he would never come back.

A STAR FOR A LADY

by DIANA PULLEIN-THOMPSON

"A GOOD 'oss" was, to George Ledbetter, like a bag of
gold. In the reign of Queen Victoria there was at least
one horse dealer in every town—and George was the
meanest of them all.

Bow-legged from hours of riding, wrinkle-faced, with
sharp blue eyes, a blob of a nose and dark, dank hair,
he was half-English, half-Irish. His father had been a
butcher, and from the age of six George had been in and
out of his father's stables, an undersized boy, quick, quiet
and crafty. He spoke little, and he was poor at school-
work, but he kept his eyes open and his ears alert, watching the farrier at work and listening to horse-talk.

By the time George was twenty-five, it was said that
he knew every trick of his trade.

If a horse was permanently lame on one foreleg, for
example, he would prick the other, so that, being lame
on both legs, the horse could not limp. To an inexpert
eye, it would then seem sound.

He would file down the teeth of old animals, to make
them appear younger, and drug lively or vicious horses
with hemp or opium so that they seemed docile when
buyers came to see them.

George dealt in most kinds of horses: hunters, ladies'
hacks, vanners, carriage horses, tram and bus horses,
ponies for governess carts, ponies for children, polo ponies
—even donkeys now and then. And if they were good-
looking, well, all the better. "Folk will always pay a bit
extra for something easy on the eye," he used to say.

But one hot day in June, George stood frowning in his
well-swept yard, looking critically at a lightly-made Irish
mare he had bought two months earlier at a London
auction.

53

"Dammit," he said to himself. "If only she were prettier she would make a fine lady's 'oss, but, as it is, she's a Plain Jane if ever there was one. She'll end up in a cab or at a livery stable, and I won't have made a penny." He sent a grain of grit spinning across the cobbled yard with the toe of one of his black boots, which were laced up to meet his gaiters.

Tied to a ring in the brick wall, the mare turned her head this way and that, her dark eyes catching the sunlight. Bright bay with black points, sharp little ears, a dainty muzzle and neat hoofs, she had a delicate look about her, which had so far prevented possible buyers coming near to paying the hundred and sixty guineas George was asking. All the ladies who had visited his yard, always in the company of gentlemen, had gone for the greys or the prettily-marked animals, turning down the Irish mare as soon as she was brought out of her stall and they observed her plainness.

"What she needs," George decided suddenly, "is a star—a white star right in the middle of her forehead. Then the ladies would be falling over each other to buy her. I could call her Starlight, that would please 'em, put her price up a tenner and she'd sell like lightning."

Smiling a little at this flash of inspiration, he put his hairy hands in his pockets, jingled two half-sovereigns together and called in a voice growing hoarse with overuse:

" 'Ere, 'Arry. Come on, look sharp!"

A stable boy of around twelve came running across the yard from the forage room, where he had been furtively chewing a wedge of tobacco. "Yessir!" He stood, looking down at the cobbles, a red-cheeked, sandy-haired, lean boy, with watery blue eyes and, in spite of his servility, a knowing look on his meagre face. It was the expression of a boy who has lived with the low and cunning from an early age and seen their ways. He trusted no one.

"That mare needs a star to set her off."

"Yessir."

"So, I want you to look slippy—slippy, d'ye hear?—

and run down to Smithy and fetch out Bob Barton, if he ain't too busy. Tell 'im I've got some business to talk with 'im. You understand?"

"Yes, mister."

"*Sir*. Don't you mister me, young scoundrel, or I'll be telling your father of you."

"Yessir!"

"Go on, then, what are you waiting for, eh?"

The boy ran off.

George smiled. He felt lord of his yard, and any sense of power pleased him. He went up to the mare, ran his hands down her legs. "Clean as a whistle," he muttered. "Not a blemish anywhere. Maybe two hundred guineas would be nearer the mark . . ."

Within fifteen minutes the stable boy came back with a giant of a man, black-haired and bearded, with big, scarred hands and a forty-five-inch chest.

"Mornin', Bob. Terrible 'ot, isn't it. Must be something 'orrible in that smithy of yours."

" 'Tis and all," agreed Bob Barton in his deep, growling voice.

After George had described the star he felt was needed to make the Irish mare more saleable, Bob went back to his forge to fetch the necessary equipment.

"Been a long time since anyone asked me to make a star," he said on his return. "But I used to be a great 'and at it five or six years ago. Farmer Griffin was mighty pleased with one I put on 'is five-year-old 'unter. Made all the difference, 'e said—sold the 'oss for two hundred guineas a year later."

As he talked, he worked. First of all the two men put a twitch on the mare's lip, so that she couldn't move without causing herself a strange, unforgettable pain. Then Bob cut four holes in her skin, so making the approximate shape of a star. Then he brought out an ivory skewer, which he used to work the skin within the area marked by the four holes, so that it was lifted away from the mare's forehead. Next, he produced two short lengths of wire and passed these diagonally across under the skin, so that there was a piece sticking out of each hole. These ends he made fast with packthread.

The mare was now in great pain; she trembled from head to foot, rolled her eyes and broke into a fearful sweat. But each time she moved or kicked, George tightened the twitch, so taking her attention away from the work of Bob's large but nimble hands. Round and round went the packthread, binding these half-inch ends of wire, until at last Bob was satisfied. Then he made a plaster of pitch—or tar, as we call it nowadays—and stuck it on the contraption of wire and thread, and motioned to George to release the twitch.

"That should make a pretty mare of 'er," he said, collecting together his tools and thread.

"Back in 'er stall, 'Arry," said George to the boy, who had been watching with that dreadful knowing look on his face.

"Let 'er 'ave just a little water, and then we'll give 'er a bran mash."

Bob, who was basically a kind man, ran his hand down the mare's neck.

"There, my little sweet'eart. All over now . . . all done. We've made a real little beauty of you. Treat her kindly, like," he said, turning to Harry. "It'll ache a little bit for a day or two, and she may feel a bit poorly."

Having seen a soldier's legs amputated without an anaesthetic in the Crimean War, he considered the mare's sufferings to be slight and bearable.

In fact, she spent three days, head to a wall, with a ceaseless throbbing between her eyes, while the bay hair between the wires died for lack of blood and fell out.

Then Bob Barton returned, came to her stall, pulled off the plaster of pitch, loosened the cord and removed the wire. And the skin and nerves felt so dead that the mare hardly moved.

"Steady now, my little darling, this will make it feel better," he crooned in his deep voice, which had quietened many a youngster frightened by the acrid smell of the smoke from its own hoofs.

Gently he poured a mixture of honey of roses and

tincture of benzoin into each hole, then rubbed the rest on the area which the pitch had held fast.

"Beautiful job," he said, standing back a little to admire his handiwork. "Bring 'er out, 'Arry, where the light's better. I reckon she's 'ad enough of this stall during the past three days." He turned to George. "Of course, there's some as use caustic, but that often turns the place bald. This be bald now, but the grey 'airs will soon be growing, stimulated by the mixture."

"Well, I pay on results," George declared firmly, a cunning expression flitting across his face. "The better the star, the better the pay."

"You always were an 'ard man," the farrier said. "Right then, I'll be back in ten days."

The mare stood outside with her head low, dazed and dejected.

"Give 'er a trot up and back. Get the blood running round 'er," ordered George. "I've never known Bob Barton fail yet."

And within ten days, sure enough, the white hairs were sprouting, and the shape of the star could be clearly seen. But the mare, who had never glimpsed her face in a mirror, knew nothing of this. She only knew that the pain was over, that her forehead felt different and that she longed for a gallop again, the turf under her hoofs, the wind in her mane and the fresh, sweet smell of the country around her.

July came, and the season of riding hacks in the Park was past, for most of the rich left London in mid-summer for airier places. But one day the head groom of a noble-man's stable came on the lookout for a lightweight horse for his master's daughter. A pretty mare, he wanted, with a look of breeding about her. He had known George Ledbetter years ago, when they had both been young men struggling to make their way, and he knew that George would not even attempt to deceive him.

They clapped a saddle on the mare and put Harry on top, for the boy could ride most animals, astride or sidesaddle—or facing the tail, for that matter—being agile as a monkey.

He showed off the mare's paces and galloped her hard, so that the head groom could see her wind was all right.

"With a bit more schooling, I reckon she'll do," the groom said eventually. "You've not tampered with her, other than the star, 'ave you? Miss Alice fancies an 'oss with a star, if it can't be a dapple grey."

"I warrant 'er sound in wind, limb and eye, and there's five gold sovereigns for you, Jack, if you can get me a hundred and ninety guineas," replied George Ledbetter, smiling his secretive smile at the thought of the profit he was about to make.

The deal was completed within three weeks; the bay mare went to roomier, lighter quarters in the nobleman's spacious yard. Bob Barton demanded, and received, two sovereigns for his work, and George Ledbetter started to look out at sales for plain horses and ponies that could be made beautiful for his own profit. He saw himself growing rich, moving to a larger house and providing his wife with a parlour maid. But Bob Barton stymied him; for, all at once, the farrier grew disgusted by the work, hated the twitch, the frightened eyes of the horses as he pushed in the ivory skewer, and the dealer's crafty, lucre-loving smile.

When all was said and done, in spite of certain coarse ways, he was a religious man, who thought of animals as "God's beasts".

" 'Tis flying in the face of nature," he announced suddenly, as he cut the fourth hole in a brown gelding's forehead. "God made this young 'oss to be plain, and who am I to know better than the Good Lord!"

He spoke emotionally, as though this sudden feeling of disgust had come as a revelation, and, with his great dark beard and shining eyes, he looked suddenly like an angry prophet. Nothing George could do, say or offer would bring him back to perform the odious operation again. The plain horses stayed plain, the bigger house was never bought, and George's wife continued to lay her own table and open her front door to the few visitors who called.

But the Irish mare prospered and grew sleek and was to be seen on most fine days cantering in the nobleman's park with the pleasant-faced Alice on her back. Her star was greatly admired for the perfection of its shape; and only four people knew the secret: the dealer, the farrier, the stable boy and the head groom.

But George Ledbetter and Bob Barton were not allowed to forget. Fate, Providence, Divine Retribution—call it what you will—saw to that.

One stormy June evening, some eleven years after the mare was sold, Bob Barton was walking up the hill to the dealer's yard to give advice on a sick horse. Now, his black beard was sprinkled with grey like a dark hedge touched with December frost. His eyes had lost a little of their extraordinary brightness, and his back had a bend in it from all the leaning over horses' hooves as he shod them. Nevertheless, he whistled cheerfully enough, and his strong legs bore his great body well. Above him, the sky was wild with skidding clouds: dark, frilled patches, interspersed with pools of brilliant blue.

"It was June," he thought, "but 'otter than now, when I starred that little bay mare for 'im. What a star that was! What a masterpiece! But 'twas a sin, surely 'twas a sin." And as he thought, he was surprised to see wisps of white vapour, like mist, only a few yards ahead of him.

"More like September than June," he decided, rubbing his eyes with those large, nimble hands. " 'Tis to be 'oped it doesn't 'erald rain, or the 'ay will be surely ruined."

But, as he came nearer the mist, it dissolved, and there, right in front of him, was the head of a horse, as though lit by heaven with a halo. A lovely head, delicate, with a fine muzzle and dilated nostrils, and eyes dark as turpentine and bright as polished mahogany, with blue in their centres, like jewels. Right between these magnificent, pleading eyes there shone a snow-white star, more shapely and perfect than any made by nature; a star which Bob Barton recognised with a stab of mingled admiration and remorse, tainted, a moment later, by fear.

"A vision! I've never 'ad a vision. But 'tis the mare. I swear 'tis the mare! The little ears, the eyes—and that look! My God, forgive us all!"

As these thoughts flashed through the farrier's mind, a trickle of sweat sprang like cold water from his forehead, and a shiver ran down his back like an attack of pins and needles. His swarthy face paled, and, looking down, he saw that his hands were trembling, as though he was possessed of the palsy.

"'Tis the mare! She's gone and died and come back to haunt us!"

He spoke aloud this time, and there was comfort in hearing his own voice.

"Whoa, my little beauty, steady there. Come on, my little sweet'eart."

His voice was like a caress, so soft and loving that it seemed to stroke, for, as he had grown older, he had come to care deeply for all living things.

He put out one roughly-hewn hand to touch, to feel, but it met nothing but air—air full of the warmth of June and the sweet scent of drying hay. He drew it back then to rub his eyes, and when he looked again the mare had gone. There was nothing but the winding road, climbing up to meet the wild evening sky.

"'Twas a vision . . . Or it may be I'm getting fancies in my middle years. Worse things 'ave 'appened to men of my age. Could be the Good Lord speaking to me. Could be I've got a screw coming loose in my greying 'ead," he whispered, trying to quell his fear.

He started to walk again and, reasoning with himself, grew calmer. What he feared most was the thought that he might be going mad, that he might end his days in the terrible, over-crowded buildings used as asylums for the insane.

By the time he had reached the dealer's yard he was feeling relaxed and surer of himself. It was a passing freak, a fancy, that was all.

George Ledbetter was leaning against a stable door; his blue eyes had grown more watery with the years, and little purple veins stood out like threads of dyed cotton on his blob of a nose.

Beside him was another man of around the same age, also with bowed legs, but with a trim figure and a small, bony face.

"Where's the sick 'oss? I've not much time to spare this night," called Bob Barton in his booming voice.

"She's been and died. Colic it was first, a twisted gut—no doubts about that. A sad business. She cost me forty guineas," replied the dealer. "But it's a blessing you've come, Bob, because there's an 'oss 'ere with a pricked 'oof, and I want the shoe off. Ted 'ere wants 'er, for the young lady who 'ad that Irish mare you put the star on. Well, she's a young mistress now, 'aving married the young Lord Mountjoy, and she liked that mare so much she said to go to the same place for an 'oss to replace it."

"The mare's dead?" Bob Barton's voice seemed a note higher than usual.

"She was getting long in the tooth," Ted said.

"When did she die?" asked Bob.

"Last Friday, eight days past. She was a beauty, gentle as a kitten, and Miss Alice fair worshipped her."

"You look pale, Bob. Anything the matter? Why, you look as though you've seen a ghost!" exclaimed the dealer. " 'Ere, let me fetch you a chair."

Bob Barton said it was just a passing fit of giddiness, and they should bring the mare out. A bit of work would do him good, and, sure enough, wrenching off the shoe brought the colour back to his face, and he was able to ease the pressure on the wound beneath.

Walking home, he hoped and prayed he would not see the Irish mare again, for now he was sure that it was her ghost which had come to him through the mist.

"The Good Lord rest her soul, if horses have souls," he muttered, making the sign of the cross.

And he never saw her again, although the ghostly sight of her was now lodged for ever in his mind, and often he dreamt of her and woke up shivering and sweating.

George Ledbetter was not so easily spared.

That night in bed, he was disturbed suddenly by his door opening and the sound of unshod hoofs on uneven boards. Sitting up and opening his eyes, he, too, saw the wisps of vapour and, through the vapour, the head of the Irish mare, and those imploring eyes, and he was all at once filled with unexpected remorse for what he had paid Bob Barton to do.

This time, the mare held the hated home-made twitch between her teeth and, rearing up, struck at him with one neat foreleg. He cowered back, his hairy hands hopelessly catching at the air, as though he could seize the twitch and gain control. He tried to shout, to scream, but his voice seemed to freeze in his throat. Yet he could hear his heart hammering and his breath coming in huge puffs, as if from Bob Barton's bellows down at the Smithy.

He felt no pain at the actual blow from the mare's hoof—just a touch, as though silken thread had passed across his brow. But a moment later a searing pain in his forehead sent him reeling back against the pillows, and his tasselled bedcap (a present from his wife), spun through the air as though thrown by unseen hands, and crashed on the floor as noisily as a saucepan lid falling on bricks.

"A nightmare?" he asked himself in the hoarsest of whispers. But no, his eyes were open and the pain was real. This was no dream; this was reality—or else he was dead and this was hell itself. Had no one else heard the clatter? Was he alone? Except for the mare and that shining white star, that head lit as though by heaven.

"Ellen! Ellen!" He found his voice at last, but it sounded like the wail of a frightened child, rather than the call of a man who owned stables full of horses, and ten acres of land.

And, hearing that cry, the mare swung round on her hocks in one graceful pirouette—and was gone. Where? Through the window? No, the window was half-closed, as before. Through the door? But there was no sound on the wooden staircase. She had gone into nothingness, and so, from nothingness, she could come again. Now there were footsteps—human footsteps.

"Whatever on earth! Whatever next! Shouting at this

62

His voice seemed to freeze in his throat . . .

time of night, when all decent folks are asleep. What's ailing you, a nightmare?"

Ellen was there in her long, white nightgown, a flickering candle in her hand. "You look like death!" she exclaimed. " 'Ere, I'll get you some water." Her grey hair was loose about her shoulders, her bony old feet bare.

"Can't you smell it?—An 'oss 'as been 'ere," said the dealer weakly, scrambling out of bed to retrieve the nightcap. And, indeed, the sweet, pungent smell of horses seemed all about the room.

"Don't be daft, it's them breeches in the chair. The smell never leaves them, does it. It's part of our life, ain't it? 'As been for years."

Ellen fetched a glass of water, scolded him for his fancies and hurried back to the comfort of her feather mattress.

George Ledbetter slept no more that night. At dawn, he rose as usual and saw in the mirror for the first time the purple bump upon his forehead, which was to fester and grow like some hideous boil, so that men shrank from him and averted their gaze, and the local doctors and chemists shook their heads in hopeless puzzlement.

"What could it be, old George Ledbetter's growth? Surely no ordinary infection, no recognisable lump?" people asked, and there was no reply at first, although suspicions were growing in minds, and there was talk in the baker's shop.

In his heart, his poor, meagre heart, which had known and given so little love, the dealer knew whence the lump had come. And Bob Barton knew also, but no one else, for the two men dared not speak for fear of being pronounced mad. Nor did they discuss the matter with each other, not wishing to put such weird and horrible thoughts into words.

In spite of days of irritation, endless poultices and hours of bathing in hot water to draw and soften it, the lump never burst. But in winter, when the first frosts silvered the dark lanes with ice, and the pale sun lay low upon the roof-tops, the swelling started to wrinkle, like an apple kept too long in a barn. And the pain and irritation stopped.

"It's going away," whispered Ellen. "It was like a curse. It 'ad me frightened. But what for? Who would want to put the curse on you, George?"

"I've always been fair and straight," her husband replied, knowing as he spoke that he was uttering a lie.

By Christmas time, the skin was flat again; the scar remained, but began to develop a positive shape, there on the centre of his forehead above the blob of a nose.

After a while, a few local boys called it mockingly "The Star of Bethlehem", and nicknamed the dealer "Bethy". But now the village adults knew better. Many had long been jealous of the dealer's financial successes, feeling them ill-deserved.

"It's one of them 'osses come back to put the mark of a curse upon 'im," some said gladly. "A warning to us all not to ill-treat God's creatures."

For by January the scar had taken its permanent shape. On that crafty forehead there stood out, like some tribal symbol, the perfect, purple outline of a star.

LISA

by DAPHNE FROOME

IT was the half term holiday, and Lisa felt so happy she fairly skipped up the two flights of stone steps to ring the bell of Miss Fraser's flat.

"I've been sent to tell Miss Fraser we've sorted out all the jumble ready for the sale," she said brightly to the strange lady who opened the door.

The lady gazed down at her blankly.

"The jumble sale for the stray animals' charity that she runs," explained Lisa patiently. "It's to be held at the scout hut at three o'clock this afternoon, and as it's one o'clock already everyone's wondering why she hasn't arrived yet."

"Oh, but Miss Fraser has suddenly gone down with 'flu. I'm waiting for the doctor now," said the strange woman. "She's quite bad, so I'm sure she wouldn't want to be bothered with jumble sales today. *I* think she does far too much charity work and tires herself out."

"I'm sorry," Lisa answered. "Is there anything I can do to help?"

"Not really," replied the woman. "She just needs to keep warm and rest."

Lisa hesitated. "She has some raffle tickets I'm supposed to collect. We're going to raffle some of the better things . . ."

"Yes, yes, I dare say." The woman looked worried. "I don't know where they are. I'm only her next-door neighbour. But you can come in and look for them if you like, only don't make a noise, Miss Fraser is asleep. There's a great pile of letters that came this morning, too—they were still on the mat when I arrived. I've put them on the desk. If any of them are to do with this charity of yours, perhaps you could deal with them."

66

Lisa tiptoed into Miss Fraser's study. She knew all the charity things were kept in there. Yes, here were the raffle tickets on the desk, with the morning's post beside them. There were a good many letters, Lisa looked through them and found two or three addressed to the animals' charity. She supposed she *ought* to open them in case they contained something urgent, about the jumble sale, for instance, and she *had* often gone through the post with Miss Fraser before.

She took up the paper knife, which was plastic and in the shape of a London sparrow, the emblem of their charity, and, feeling quite important, she began to slit open the envelopes.

The contents seemed to be very disappointing: just advertisements, or bills. But what was this last one, that bulged so very interestingly? It was a letter on blue note-paper and, as Lisa unfolded it, a key dropped out.

"Dear Dolly," it read. (Lisa stifled a giggle; she could never have imagined anyone addressing Miss Fraser, who was tall and angular and had a habit of looking at you severely through large spectacles, as "Dolly".) "We left in such a hurry for our tour of the Lake District that I quite neglected to answer your request for something for your sale. I haven't any jumble, but there are four quite valuable plates, worth at least five pounds each, which I would be happy for you to collect from 3, Regency Grove. You will find them in the box-room on the second floor, between the two bedrooms. They are in a large brown paper carrier-bag, so you can't fail to see them. Back in two weeks, key enclosed. Jane Benson."

Lisa knew 3, Regency Grove. She had been there to collect jumble before. It was right in the centre of the City, not far from Bow Church, but quite a short journey by bus from Miss Fraser's flat. If she went at once she could collect the plates and be back easily before the beginning of the sale, and how pleased everyone would be if she turned up with four plates worth five pounds each. Twenty pounds! That would push the takings up.

"Are you all right, dear?" asked Miss Fraser's neighbour, behind her.

"Yes, thank you," answered Lisa. "I've found the raffle tickets and opened the charity letters——"

"Ah, that sounds like the doctor now; you'd better go."

Lisa found herself outside the flat.

Feeling quite excited, she hurried along the road and caught the bus into the City. This jumble sale was proving far more interesting that she had imagined; in fact, the stray animals' charity work seemed to get more and more interesting all the time, and next week the helpers were actually to take part in the procession at the Lord Mayor's Show. Miss Fraser kept on about what a wonderful advertisement it would be for the charity, and, though Lisa had to agree, she could not help also thinking, secretly to herself, how thrilling it would be to travel along on the float behind the fine carriages of the Lord Mayor and all the important London people, with the crowds cheering.

As she walked along Cheapside towards Bow Church, the clock was just striking two and a slight November mist was making everything look smudgy and nicer than it really was. Not that Lisa did not like London. She had been born in the city and could not imagine living anywhere else. She liked it when it was noisy and bustling, and now, when it was sleeping in its Saturday afternoon quiet.

She made her way along the side streets that led to Regency Grove. It was a small, out of the way cul-de-sac set in among tall new buildings, like a bit of the past that had somehow been forgotten. In fact, Lisa noticed that all the other houses in Regency Grove seemed to be offices now. It must have been much nicer when they were first built in Regency days and all occupied by grand families, she thought. Not that the Bensons' house did not still look prosperous, even with the windows all firmly closed, the brass knocker and letterbox dull and the short path leading in through the wrought iron gate from the pavement dusty and unswept. Perhaps it had something to do with the two supercilious and dignified looking gargoyles, one each side, scowling down from the tops of the gate-posts. They seemed to be regarding her very suspiciously, so she ran past them quickly and put the key in the lock of the heavy front door. She suddenly felt very grand, walking in. "Just as if I was very wealthy and lived here," she thought, and she was sorry there was no one about to watch her go in and close the heavy door behind her.

The house had a slightly frightening, shut up, deserted feeling, but, making her way up the wide, curving staircase, Lisa soon found the box-room. The door was open, revealing a small room of little use for anything, since the window had been bricked up in the days of the window tax, and very different from all the other beautifully furnished rooms in the house. Lisa switched on the light, went in and automatically pushed the door shut behind her. Yes, there was the carrier-bag. She looked inside, and there were the plates. She lifted them out and laid them on the floor. They were fine china and very, very pretty, with an intricate pattern in gold around the edges. She put them carefully back in the bag and turned to go.

She had forgotten she had shut the door. She looked for the handle. Bother, she thought, it seemed to be missing. She began to hunt round for it. It was not lying about anywhere, and there were no cupboards it could be in. In fact, the room was quite bare except for a rickety-looking wooden chair and a couple of cardboard boxes, one containing an old straw hat and the other a few out-dated and uninteresting looking magazines.

"Bother!" she exclaimed, aloud this time. She put down the plates and hammered on the door. It was a very solid door, smooth and well-fitting, so there was no way of getting a grip on it from the inside. It refused to budge. Lisa wished the light was brighter so she could see better. Even though it had no shade it was very dim. The walls, with their faded, floral-patterned paper, looked as solid as the door, the ceiling was of heavy plaster, and the floor was thick boarding.

She was a prisoner; there was no way out unless she could batter down the door.

She took up the rickety chair, held it firmly by the back and swung it sideways at the door. The back broke off and the rest of the chair fell with a crash to the floor, but, except for a few faint marks, the door remained unscathed.

Lisa began to shout and scream. She went on screaming until her voice was hoarse, but no one answered. Indeed, who was to come to her rescue, she thought, as she collapsed on to the remains of the chair, on a Saturday afternoon in the deserted City, where she was surrounded by empty offices that would remain unoccupied until Monday? "And even on Monday, if there did happen to be anyone passing, who could possibly hear me," she wondered, "in a room without a window, so well shut up, at the back of the house?"

"Don't lose your head, Lisa," she instructed herself as bravely as she could. "Someone's bound to find you sooner or later." But no one knew where she was, and the Bensons would be away for ages. "Back in two weeks," they had said in their letter. What a fix to get herself into! And only a little while ago she had been so very happy. This time yesterday she had been in the car with Mum and Dad, driving round the route of the Lord Mayor's Show.

"This is where you'll be riding," her father had said, "with Mum and me cheering you on."

They had finished the outing by going up on to Hampstead Heath, and Lisa remembered asking how long there had been Lord Mayors in London.

Dad, who, being a Cockney, seemed to know everything about London, had answered: "Since the Middle Ages—there were Lord Mayors long before the time of Richard Whittington. It's nearly six hundred years, you know, since he sat over there on Highgate Hill and heard Bow bells pealing, calling him back to London."

"Dick Whittington and his cat? I didn't know they lived as long ago as that," she had answered.

"Bless me, what do they teach you at that smart school of yours? As Lord Mayor he served three kings—Richard II, Henry IV and Henry V. Difficult times they were, what with the fighting and feuding—they say pirates, too, often came up the Thames in those days."

70

Difficult times! She reckoned Sir Richard Whittington had never got himself into a situation as difficult as this.

She fumbled in her pocket and found the Bensons' letter and key, a handkerchief, the raffle tickets, some money and half a bar of chocolate.

"That won't last long," she thought. "I'd better keep it for a bit. Oh, what *am* I to do?"

Her shoulders drooped dejectedly. "Perhaps I could pass the time by counting," she thought. "When they find me I can say how many I've got up to, and if it's millions it'll sound terribly impressive. But if it was millions, that would mean I had been here for days and days!" She decided it was better not to count after all.

In the end she just stared at nothing, and, as the minutes dragged into hours, she even gave up glancing at her watch. The jumble sale must have ended ages ago, she thought, and everyone would be wondering whatever had become of her, and why she had not returned after collecting the raffle tickets.

The house was terribly silent except for occasional strange creaking sounds, which made it rather creepy. Then, suddenly, Lisa thought she heard bells ringing. At first they began quietly, and she thought it must be some trick played by her overwrought senses, but as the sound grew louder and louder they seemed to be ringing from everywhere in the room, from the walls, from the floor, from the ceiling, jangling through her head until Lisa felt she could bear the terrible sound no longer.

"The place must be haunted," she thought. "I can't stand it!" she cried out loud.

As if in answer to her cry, the noise gradually subsided, as though all the bells had been loaded on to a giant truck and slowly driven away. Then she heard the sound of midnight striking. She was trembling, shivering . . .

Lisa spent several minutes trying to focus her eyes on the cat which seemed to be crouched in the far corner of the room. She found it almost impossible to tell where his black fur ended and the shadows began.

They gazed at each other for a very long time. His

71

eyes seemed to gather up the faint light from the bare electric light bulb, dye it green, and send it on to Lisa in a long, leisurely stare. She noticed he had one white whisker. He busied himself licking each paw in turn, stopping to eye her inquisitively from time to time.

After a while he stood up on all fours, stretched, and suddenly, without any warning, sidled very deliberately across the room, leapt lightly towards the wall, and disappeared.

Lisa rubbed her eyes. Had he gone through the wall—or simply vanished? "He can't have gone through the wall . . . it's solid," she told herself.

She was quite baffled, and still very shaken, too, after the deafening clamour of the bells. She staggered to her feet, went over to the wall, and looked at the place where he had disappeared. Then she searched carefully around the room. Except for the bricked-up window it was ordinary enough. "I must be going mad," she thought. "It's the shock of all this. I must try to keep calm."

In spite of all her brave intentions, she decided that she must have started to cry at this stage, because when she caught sight of the cat again, edging slowly along the same bit of the wall as before, his shape looked more blurred and uncertain than ever.

He did not hesitate this time, but bounded straight across the floor, travelling purposefully towards her. He glanced at her once before vanishing through the wall again.

She waited a while but he did not return.

Lisa suddenly felt terribly lonely. She began to examine much more thoroughly the area where he had disappeared. When she tapped it, it made a curious sound, wooden and hollow, different from the dull thud of the surrounding brick.

"Perhaps it's not as solid as I thought," she said to herself, and, seizing the remains of the chair, she struck with all her might. Nothing happened at first, but then suddenly, with a dull, muffled, splintering noise, the chair crashed through. She peered into the opening, attacked it again with the by now very battered chair, and peered

72

again. It was a chimney! She was at first pleased and then bitterly disappointed, but she went on tearing away the wallpaper, breaking down the thin boarding, until the remains of a fireplace appeared. It was better than doing nothing.

And then, to her surprise, she noticed the cat again. He leapt, almost flew, she thought, across the few feet between them, landed beside her, and began to scrabble over the broken bricks and soot that had fallen down over the years, and the bits of wood and paper that Lisa had torn away, into the chimney itself. She peered up after him. It was very dark and he was little more than an indistinct blur anyway, but she was just in time to notice his dim shape disappearing up the narrow chimney.

"Oh, puss," she called, "I wish I knew what you were up to."

To her surprise, the cat suddenly came back down again and sat for a moment looking almost solid, eyeing her with just the kind of stare—reproachful with a peppering of impatient sternness—that Lisa remembered seeing on Miss Fraser's face when one of the charity helpers was being particularly stupid.

Then he began his upward journey again.

Lisa wondered whether to try to follow him. "Supposing I get stuck?" she thought. "It does look so terribly narrow. Oh, anything's better than staying in this awful room," she decided, and she shovelled away the debris in the fireplace as quickly as she could and scrambled in after him. It really was very dark, and at that moment she could think of nothing more difficult than trying to follow the progress of the ghost of a black cat up a soot-grimed chimney in the dark. She squeezed further in. There seemed to be a bend about five feet from the ground, which curved backwards into a kind of platform. Lisa twisted round with considerable difficulty, and, pushing with her feet, hauled herself up on to the ledge. The cat was obviously some way ahead of her. "Which is just as well," she mused, "for there would never be room for us both."

She felt around in the darkness. The chimney seemed

to go off to the side now, and she crawled along, blinking the dust out of her eyes. The passage turned to the left, and suddenly became very wide and spacious as a number of other chimneys joined it. Looking up towards the top, which now seemed not much more than a few feet away, she could see quite clearly the outline of the stack against the open sky. A little way above her, the cat, which had been sitting perched on a kind of foothold, jumped up easily on to another, then another, until, when he had almost reached the top, he stopped and waited. Lisa could almost feel him willing her upwards. "They're steps!" she shouted. "Steps!" But then she hesitated. Supposing some should be broken? ("You can always go back, silly," she chided herself.) Or that they should give way beneath her weight? ("Well, I'll just have to test each one.") The sides of the chimney were sharp to her hands and some-times crumbled at her touch, but the old brick steps, which, she thought, must once have been used by chimney-sweeps, held.

She looked up once. Yes, the cat was still there. "All right, mog, I'm doing my best," she called breathlessly. "I might not be as light and wispy as you, but if you can do it, so can I."

Lisa needed all her strength to finish her climb and clamber out on to the roof. Once there, she stood still for a very long time. She had never before felt so grateful to be breathing fresh air, and the space between her and the hazy moon seemed endless.

The cat waited, rather impatiently, she thought, at the edge of the gutter.

Lisa tried the slates cautiously, then she went slowly down them towards the place where the cat was waiting. There, zig-zagging down from the roof, was a fire-escape leading to the ground. Lisa's legs felt very shaky beneath her as she climbed down the iron steps, but eventually she reached the gate and went through on to the pavement.

She leant against the railings and closed her eyes.

When she opened them again she could just make out the shadowy figure of a horseman cantering towards her through the mist; and, as he approached, she heard the bells begin to peal again, the sound seeming to gather in the little cul-de-sac, echoing around her, growing louder and louder. But she hardly felt frightened any more.

The man reined in his horse opposite Lisa, turned and bowed gently towards her, and as he did so she caught a glimpse of the great gold chain of the Lord Mayor of London; then he extended his arm to the cat, which jumped up in front of him, and horse, rider and cat seemed gradually to become part of the mist. By the time they had disappeared altogether, it was silent again in the street.

"And after all that I didn't remember the plates," thought Lisa.

She was travelling along in the procession on the stray animals' charity float, which really did look splendidly gay. It was a wonderful pageant: there were the Lord Mayor and the aldermen in splendid coaches, the horses, the people. Lisa caught a glimpse of her parents. They had somehow managed at the last minute to find special places next to Miss Fraser, who looked pale but recovered, on the Mansion House balcony. They waved enthusiastically; she waved back. The band was playing a stirring march. Then the rain, slight at first, turned into a sudden downpour. It gathered on the rim of Lisa's new hat, bought specially for the occasion, and then, spilling off, ran down between her neck and the collar of her new, matching coat. Her skirt began to cling, sodden, to her legs, her feet slopped about in her shoes as she moved. She waved to the girl opposite, whose hair was flattened wetly to her head. The girl grinned back. The band was playing even louder now, the people cheering them on. Lisa had never felt so exhilarated in her life.

Her father stood watching her from the balcony. He was very pleased to see Lisa looking so fit. When she had returned from her adventure she had been delirious with fright, insisting that she had heard Bow bells pealing in the middle of the night, and had been saved by Dick Whittington's cat. He had doubted very much if she would be well enough to join in today's festivities. But there she was, seemingly without any after-effects at all. He really felt very proud that she had kept her head and reasoned out the only possible way of escape so cleverly . . .

Suddenly he saw a black cat standing proudly beside Lisa, right on the front of the float. A black cat with one white whisker, and, in spite of the rain, very fluffy and quite, quite, dry. The cat caught his eye and winked knowingly before fading slowly into nothingness.

CHILD OF THE FUTURE

by JOHN DUNCAN

REBECCA ran lightly up the wide staircase and looked out of the upper landing window into the garden below. "That will need a lot of work," she said aloud, smiling at the estate agent's description on the sheet of paper. "'Mature garden', indeed. 'Overgrown' would be a better description."

Rebecca glanced at her watch. Her parents would be arriving in about an hour, and that gave her plenty of time to look over the house.

How many houses had they viewed in the last few hectic days since they had decided to move to the West Country? She shook her head and smiled. House-hunting was fun, anyway.

"This house was once the residence of the Duke of Knowle-Seymour, and it was built to his own design," the estate agents had written. "There are ten bedrooms, five reception rooms and a servant's annexe with three bedrooms, etc."

"This must be the master bedroom," Rebecca said to herself, pushing back the large double doors. She went into the room and opened the tall wooden shutters, allowing the dusty sunlight to tumble into the room. "Twenty-four feet by sixteen feet," she read aloud. "That's not right, surely."

She paced the room twice and arrived at the conclusion that the master bedroom must be elsewhere; yet the hanging wardrobe, the servant's bell sash and the Italian marble fireplace were all described accurately on the paper. Furrowing her brow, she went on to the landing and glanced at the other bedroom doors.

The landing was L-shaped, and she counted the doors,

ticking off each room as she walked by. "It's no use," she sighed, after a frustrating ten minutes trying to work out the positioning of the rooms, "I'll have to get the tape measure from the car."

Frozen, stony faces stared at her as she ran down the stairs under the disapproving portraits of people in old-fashioned dress.

Reaching her small red car, parked under a mimosa tree, Rebecca collected her tape measure and returned to the house, noting that there were five chimney stacks on each branch of the building; ten altogether.

"What a swizzle," she said as she rechecked her measurement of the "master bedroom". "This room is only eighteen feet by sixteen." Upon checking the adjoining room, she found that there was just over six feet difference in the measurements the estate agents had recorded, and the actual measurements of the room.

"That's twelve feet," she calculated. "Where have I made the mistake? One can't mislay a room." She tapped the wall with her pencil and was surprised to hear the hollow, empty sound it made. "This is only a partition wall. But I wonder where the door to this extra room is?"

She leaned out of the window and tried to locate the window of the extra room, and she felt along the adjoining walls in both the bedrooms to see if there was a concealed opening. She hoped there was. How excited her mother and father would be if they were to find a house with a secret room.

Finally, Rebecca went out into the hall and examined the area of wall where she thought a door ought to be. There was a massive oil painting of a man in red clothing, and Rebecca pulled it away from the wall. But it was not until she had pulled it some distance that she realised the painting was, in fact, a door.

"A secret room!" she breathed, ducking her head through the dark doorway. Perhaps she would be allowed to have the room to study in if she passed the entrance examination to become a nurse.

"Close the door," a voice said imperiously.

"Mum?" Rebecca jumped at the sound. "What are

78

"Close the door," a voice said imperiously.

you doing here? I thought you were coming on the bus with Dad, later on this afternoon."

The room appeared to light up, like a theatre when the performance is finished, and Rebecca saw that dozens of candles were flickering busily in a glass chandelier.

At the far end of the room stood a woman, her hair piled outrageously high on her head.

"Mum?" Rebecca approached the woman. "Is that you, Mum? Please don't play games with me. I'm a bit frightened."

A cold draught of air slithered down Rebecca's neck as the woman turned to face her.

"I asked you to close the door, child," she said severely. "Close the door, I say. You know how cold your poor mama becomes when the door is left ajar."

Still keeping her eyes on the woman, who resembled her own mother so much, Rebecca pulled the door shut and stepped into the room.

Books lined the walls, and there was an antique desk to the left of the fireplace. The woman was dressed in a long silk gown and her face was garishly rouged.

"Rebecca." She surveyed the girl with annoyance. "Whatever is the matter with you, child? It seems to me you have been acting very strangely of late. It's almost as if you weren't really with us half the time."

"Where did you get the costume?" Rebecca asked, venturing a pace or two nearer so that she could examine the woman more closely. Yet somehow she knew that the figure standing near the fireplace was not, in fact, her mother . . . although she looked so much like her, and the voice was the same. Rebecca put her hand to her head, wondering if it was a dream. Then she noticed that she was no longer wearing her watch. Not only that, but she seemed to be dressed in similar design and fashion to the other woman.

"My dress!" she gasped.

"And what is wrong with your dress?" the woman snapped as she delicately picked up a small log and placed it on the roaring fire.

"*I'm* the one who should be asking questions," Rebecca

thought, panic-stricken. "This isn't happening to me. It can't be happening." She stared at the woman. "Who are you?" she asked.

"Who am I?" The woman laughed shrilly. "Who am I? Why, Rebecca my dear, you must have a fever. I am your mother."

"But your clothes, this house . . . How did you get here?"

"I think you ought to retire to your bedroom, child." The woman apparently tired of the conversation. "I will send a coach for Doctor Harris. He'll probably have to bleed you again."

"Bleed me?"

"Obviously you have some poison in your system, Rebecca, and the good doctor will know what to do."

Rebecca gaped and backed away. It was like "Alice Through the Looking-Glass". What was happening to her?

"Do you live here?" she asked, hastily adding: "I mean, do you only live in this one room?"

"My . . . Oh, my!" The woman came across the room and peered intently into Rebecca's face. "The poor girl is losing her reason. Such silly questions. You know that your father had this room built especially for me because I feel the cold so much. You know that I am your mother." The woman examined Rebecca's face and put her hand out to feel her forehead.

"Don't touch me!" Rebecca cried, stepping back from the icy fingers. "You are not my mother!"

"Rebecca, *dear*," the woman coaxed, "you must not say such things or people will think that you are mad. Your father will never allow me to keep you in the house if he thinks you have lost your reason. He loathes illness of any kind—you would have to be sent to Bedlam."

"Bedlam?"

"The priory of Bethlehem at Bishopsgate, dear, where they keep people who are mad."

"Mad?" Rebecca asked weakly. She stared at the fire and felt the fierce heat of the flames as they devoured the tiny logs, and she put out a hand to touch the solid wall behind her back. "I am not mad," she said defiantly. "I came here to view this house, and my mother and father will be arriving shortly. They are looking at some properties in Newton Dyneswell first."

"Newton Dyneswell?" The woman laughed. "But there are only fields at Newton Dyneswell, child. Whatever made you say a thing like that?"

"The estate agent knows that I'm here." Rebecca slid along the wall, trying to place some distance between the woman and herself.

"Estate agent?" The woman shook her head slowly, so that the high confection of powdered hair would not be disarranged by the action.

"I know what you're doing," Rebecca said firmly. "You're trying to make me believe I'm mad. It's a joke, but you won't convince me." She rushed over to a chair, where she could see the corner of a newspaper protruding from behind a cushion. "Here," she cried, "now we shall see what the date is."

She stared at the single sheet of paper. There was a drawing on the page, and Rebecca read a passage aloud. She stood there, hypnotised by what she was saying.

"And it is further reported that Lord North has been taken ill with the shock of the news that General Burgoyne surrendered his men to General Gates . . ."

"That's enough, Rebecca," the woman snapped, taking the newspaper from her. "You know that your father would disapprove of you reading such things."

"The American War of Independence;" Rebecca cried. "But that was two hundred years ago."

"Seven weeks ago," the woman corrected.

Suddenly Rebecca broke down and began to sob. It was all too much.

"There, there, child." The woman was at her side instantly. "You must not distress yourself about the loss of one colony. The King will not allow such insubordination to continue for long."

"Please," Rebecca sobbed, "please stop it. Tell me the truth. Who are you?"

"Hush, child." The woman stroked Rebecca's forehead with icy fingers, and she shuddered at the touch.

"Listen." Rebecca shook the fingers from her head and stood up to face the woman. "It's not seventeen-seventy something. You can't fool me. I came here with a watch on my wrist. I drove a car. I . . ."

The woman rose from the chair, her eyes blazing angrily. "You are not to get yourself in a state, Rebecca," she admonished. "I will not hear this nonsense. You are talking gibberish."

"Then tell me you don't know what a radio is and a telephone and aeroplanes and television. Tell me that men have not walked on the moon, that ships don't travel under the sea and that people don't . . ."

A stinging slap silenced her.

"Stop it!" the woman shouted. "You know what happened the last time you had one of your attacks."

The slap seemed to drain all the anger and energy out of Rebecca and she suddenly felt sorry for the woman, who seemed to be genuinely worried about her.

"Look," she said soberly. "I don't know what has happened, but something very strange is going on. I don't belong here. I live in a time that is two hundred years away. Men have progressed; they do things that you would not ever dream possible." She wanted to console the woman, but she could not bring herself to touch her.

"Men walking on the moon . . ." the woman said. "How is that possible, child? Oh, I know you have been right before, but the things you are saying are just too fantastic to be true."

"I was right before?" Rebecca asked. "What did I say? I don't even remember having talked to you before."

"Captain Cook," the woman replied. "You were right about this discovery of a new land. You were even right when you said it would be called New South Wales. However, it is ridiculous to——"

"But I didn't talk about Captain Cook!" Rebecca exploded. "He's just a figure in our history books at school."

"School?"

"Yes, school. I passed all my exams, and history was

one of my best subjects, so I know what I'm talking about.
Captain Cook was killed at Owhyhee on February 14th,
1779, and England went to war with Spain on June the
16th."

"But how can you know that?" the woman cried. "It's
1777 now. How can you know what is going to happen in
the future?"

"I live in the future." Rebecca stared wildly around
the room. "And I must get back. I don't belong here with
you."

"Now, Rebecca." The woman's voice held a warning in
it. "Don't you start off again. We don't want to have
another of your tantrums, or I will have to strap you
tightly so that you cannot harm yourself."

"I'm all right." Rebecca spoke evenly, trying to make
her way to the door. "Please leave me alone. I'll be fine
in a moment."

The woman appeared to relax, and Rebecca took
advantage of the moment to rush for the door.

"Stop! Rebecca!"

Almost crying with the effort, Rebecca gripped
the ornate brass door handle and wrenched the door
open.

"Don't go!" The woman's voice sounded so pitiful
that Rebecca hesitated for a brief moment.

"I must," she said, gritting her teeth to keep control of
herself.

The woman was standing near the fire, and a log spat
hot cinders out on to the carpet.

"There's ash on the carpet," said Rebecca, pointing.
Then, as the woman looked down, she pulled the door shut
and ran out on to the landing.

A blast of warm air seemed to slap her in the face,
frightening her and making her break into a run.

"Rebecca . . . Rebecca!" the woman's voice came
echoing after her.

"Go away!" Rebecca cried.

"Rebecca . . . Rebecca!"

Past the oil paintings, down the stairs . . .

"Rebecca, Rebecca!" There was an evil hint of laughter

in the voice, and Rebecca tried to block out the sound as she fumbled with the handle of the front door.

"Rebecca!" The voice seemed nearer.

"Rebecca! Don't leave me, my darling!"

Fingers curled around the doorknob. Frozen fingers that seemed unable to turn it.

"Rebecca, come back to me! Come back to your mother, my child."

"You're not my mother!" Rebecca shrieked as the door swung suddenly open. And there, before her, stood her mother.

Rebecca screamed.

All the force she was able to muster went into that agonising scream; a scream that drove all the breath from her lungs and all the energy from her limbs. She collapsed, grateful and spent, into the blackness of her mother's arms.

"She's coming round," the voice said above the hum of the car engine. "Silly girl." It was her father's voice. "I told her not to view houses on her own. She's far too imaginative and easily frightened."

"All the same," said Rebecca's mother, wiping her daughter's face with a cool flannel, "I didn't like the place very much. It was spooky and I—well, I had the strange feeling that I had been there before."

"Stuff and nonsense!" Rebecca's father replied, pulling the car over sharply to avoid an oncoming fire engine. "Dammit," he said, watching the engine career around the corner, "that was close. We could have been killed."

Rebecca sat up and stared through the back window. "It's going to that house," she said dumbly. "A log fell out of the fire."

"Fire, darling?" Rebecca's mother asked. "Why should there be a fire in an empty house?"

"There was," Rebecca replied. "Look! Stop the car, Daddy!"

Far below them in the valley, under a pall of grey smoke, the house was burning. "It was an evil place," Rebecca said as she watched the flames leap high.

Then, as they watched the firemen rush around the house like busy ants, Rebecca told them of her experience. As she was about to finish, she saw that her father was staring at her.

"You must have been dreaming, Rebecca," he said. "Maybe you're ill." He started the car. "Look, I'm going to take you to the hospital. There's something wrong with you."

"No," her mother said firmly. "I think we had all better go home and try to forget about this."

"But . . . Aren't you worried about her?"

"We are going home," Rebecca's mother insisted. "And we will throw this away." She opened the window and, taking the crumpled sheet of paper from Rebecca's hand, she tossed it out. "Drive us home, please," she said. "There's something evil about this place."

Rebecca snuggled against her mother, the way she used to when she was a child, and the car sped away as the flames devoured the house in the valley below.

The wind snatched the sheet of paper and tossed it high in the air, playing with it noisily for a while, then tiring of the game. Exhausted, the paper fell on to the grass, rolled and rustled and anchored itself to a granite cross.

The wind crept over the hedge and whistled casually through the gravestones, lifting the edge of the sheet of paper to read the inscription that was carved on the tombstone.

Here lies poor Rebecca,
Sweet Peace at last.
Child of the Future,
Gone home to rest.

Then the wind tore angrily at the sheet of paper and threw it down into the valley, where the flames of the house devoured it.

THE PHANTOM PIRATES

by RICK FERREIRA

EVERY schoolboy on Tomango knew the legend of Captain Skull and his band of bloodthirsty pirates.

It told how once, about two centuries ago, Tomango had been the Captain's favourite island in the West Indies. With its sheltered bay, it provided a safe place for him to hide his ship . . . then, unmolested, the pirates could bury their stolen treasure, deep in the white sand of the beach, just beyond the tumbling blue waves of the Caribbean sea.

And the Captain himself had been a fearsome sight to behold!

Over his head he always wore a black hood. On it there had been the outline and features of a grinning skull, painted white, with the Captain's crazed black eyes gleaming through the eye-slits . . .

So ran the legend.

And Christopher and Jonah had heard it all ever since they could remember. And the other part, too—the part that the boys had always scoffed at—that on the first night of each full moon, Captain Skull and his crew returned to the beach to dig up their treasure chests, then to check by moonlight the gold and silver coins, the gem-stones and the pearls, big as pigeon's eggs. And then were furious if their treasure had been disturbed. Apparently, if there was one thing Captain Skull and his pirates couldn't stand, it was thieves!

And tonight—with a gigantic full moon riding high and clear above the sea and the coconut palms—*tonight*, Christopher and Jonah had decided that the time had come to investigate the old legend, once and for all. They both felt brave enough and, anyway, it was just an old island tale . . .

But when the big alarm clock with the double copper bells woke them up with its racket, it was well after midnight. So the boys argued breathlessly, racing along in the moonlight, heading for the clump of coconut trees and the winding path that led steeply down to the beach.

"You set that clock, not me," Jonah protested. "Hold it, Masta Chris . . . I drop my piece of sugar-cane!" Jonah's thin legs braked to a halt while his eyes searched the ground, almost day-bright by the light of the moon.

"How can you think of chewing sugar-cane *now*?" And Christopher's pyjama clad legs kept on racing. "We're already too late. See you on the beach, *glutton*!"

"Found it!" Jonah cried, hitching up the old shorts he slept in. Then he was back in his stride, racing after Christopher.

Being ten years old was the only thing the boys had in common. Blonde, chubby Christopher was English, and Tomango had been his adopted home since he was two and his widowed father had taken up the post of Medical Superintendent on the island. Jonah was a native, and he was shiny black and a compulsive eater. But he was still the thinnest ten-year-old on Tomango.

The boys raced on through the warm night, through the sad sighing of the coconut trees, and the sound of the sea grew louder as they came nearer. They reached the headland together, breathless and gasping, with Jonah sucking noisily away on his stick of sugar-cane. And they were just about to plunge down the familiar steep path to the beach, when they stopped. Utterly frozen—like two gilded statues in the moonlight—they stood, while their eyes stared unblinking at the scene on the beach below.

For the pirates *were* there!

Toiling away just beyond the reach of the waves, and buffeted by the winds from the sea, some were bending over a vast sea-chest, it's heavy lid thrown back, while they checked its precious contents. A dozen others were using wide shovels to flatten another section of the beach . . . where, presumably, another chest had been checked

88

and reburied. They seemed surly and suspicious—and looked smelly, too, Christopher thought—and all were busy.

All but Captain Skull.

He was standing guard, with a hand on the head of his cutlass and a murderous-looking pistol levelled at his men. And Captain Skull looked exactly as the boys had imagined he would. Except in just one terrifying detail. Even from the height where they stood, Christopher and Jonah could see that the Captain's head was no longer hidden by the black hood with the skull bones painted in white. Christopher's teeth started rattling like a bag of marbles, and Jonah choked on his stick of sugarcane——

For now, Captain Skull truly deserved his name. His head *was* a real, grinning skull of white, bleached bones!

And at that very moment the skull swung up and away from the beach, searching out the two boys bathed in moonlight, high up on the headland.

Christopher and Jonah stood, helpless and unmoving, while the gaping eye-sockets of Captain Skull stayed trained on them, like a deadly double-barrelled shotgun. Then they watched the grinning jaws swing open . . .

"Blasted spies!" the Captain roared. "Up above, lads!"

And with his cry, a hurricane of sound came rushing up from the beach: the clang of spades thrown hastily down, the thud of sea-boots pounding across the sand. Then the pirates were jostling and pushing and swearing . . . all anxious to scramble up the steep path to the headland and capture the boys. And Captain Skull pointed with the cutlass he had drawn from his waistband, and the moonlight that filled his eye-sockets glinted wickedly on the naked blade.

"Up there! We need cabin boys! Get 'em both!"

But life and motion had come back to Christopher and Jonah. A second later they had turned and were running with the speed only terror can inspire. Back through the coconut trees they raced, back along the

89

beach road, then down the long rough lane that led to the bungalow.

They ducked under the verandah rail, then their bare feet were slapping the wooden floor as they sped for the safety of their bedroom. Then they were in the bedroom, with the door slammed shut. Christopher tumbled headlong into his bed, and Jonah made a flying leap for the rope hammock he slept in.

And Jonah promptly fell out. He lay on the floor and laughed, slightly hysterical and filled with relief. Christopher sat up in bed and laughed, too. But it was quite a while before the boys could fall asleep again.

Salome woke them by throwing open the wooden shutters, and the sunlight poured into the bedroom like yellow paint from a can. Salome was Jonah's mother. She was also housekeeper to Christopher and his father, and she ran the bungalow with bustling good humour. And great firmness.

She was firm now.

"Why you two boys sleep so late? You talk and talk all night, I'll bet. Up, Masta Chris! Your Dad staying at the hospital for the next two nights and he said you better be good!" She trundled over to Jonah's hammock and shook it with a massive arm. "Out of that hammock, lazybones! And Jonah, see you feed them hens before breakfast . . ." Then Salome was gone and the wooden floor of the bedroom stopped its alarming creaking.

The boys never disobeyed Salome.

Ten minutes later, Jonah was throwing corn to a bunch of clucking hens, and Christopher was walking on the very beach where Captain Skull and his pirates had been so busy last night. In the bright sunshine, Christopher felt none of the blind terror that had made him and Jonah race so madly back to the bungalow.

And then he saw the coin.

It was a fat, round, gold coin, glinting in the morning sun, and lying next to a dried branch from a coconut tree. Christopher broke into a run, his blue eyes wide with surprise and delight.

"Whoopee!" he yelled as he scooped the coin up from the sand. And though the sand was already warm, the coin felt heavy and cold, but Christopher hardly noticed that. He clutched it so tightly that his fist ached, as he raced back across the sand and scrambled up the path to the headland.

He was completely winded when he found Jonah at the rear of the bungalow, shooing half a dozen hens back into the hen-house. "All going to lay eggs today," Jonah said with satisfaction. The thought of anything edible always gave Jonah a warm, secure feeling. "You look excited. What's up?"

Christopher took a deep breath, then he opened his right hand. It was a great, dramatic moment. "Look, Jonah! *Look* . . ."

Jonah looked. Jonah swallowed very loudly and took a step backwards. "That there is pirate gold! The good Lord protect you now . . ."

"*Me?* Gosh! Oh, Jonah . . . I—I forgot! I was so excited . . ."

"But you crazy? Like me, you know the other part of the story . . . *never pick up pirate money from the beach.* You know now that them dead pirates will come to you to get their coin? What'll you do then?" Fearful though he was, Jonah found that he was rather enjoying himself. "And no good you taking it back to the beach, either. *You* picked it up . . . now they must punish you!"

Chistopher listened, aghast. "You—you think they will come—*tonight*?"

"Sure as dark!" Jonah said, then he remembered that Christopher was his friend. His best friend. "Say! Why don't we do see Mister Hippy Harry right now? No—after breakfast! But you say nothing to my ma about your pirate money. She want to put gold on all her teeth. Any gold. Even pirate money gold!"

Christopher managed a wan smile.

He knew all about Salome's obsession to cover every tooth with a thin gold cap. Her wide smile was already half gold. "Hippy Harry will know what to do, won't he,

Jonah? He's so clever. He knows almost everything. What do you think?"

"I think . . . when he knows you is in mortal danger, he'll help." That sounded very reassuring, until Jonah ruined it all by saying: "We got fried pork for breakfast . . . just you *smell*!"

And at that moment Salome's great head came out of the kitchen window, and the sunlight caught the gold caps already in her mouth. "You boys come in now. It's ready."

Jonah put a wiry arm around Christopher's shoulder. "Anything you don't want . . . you just put on my plate, O.K.?"

"O.K.," Christopher said gloomily. "But how you can think of your belly at a time like this, I just don't know . . ."

The sun was a hot blaze in the sky when they finally got to Hippy Harry's shack, high in the hills above the town. The shack looked a part of the fern-covered hillside, as if it had grown out of the soil. It was ramshackle and wooden, with a thatched roof of coconut branches. It nestled deep in a small forest of towering bamboo trees.

It looked spooky even in brilliant sunlight.

"Masta Chris . . . you go on in and tell about the gold money. I'll just climb the mango tree at the back and bring you in——"

"No you *don't*!" Christopher grabbed hold of Jonah's thin arm, and together the two boys walked between the row of giant sunflower trees up to the half-open door.

Inside they found Hippy Harry.

The middle-aged Englishman was tanned to a deep coppery colour and he wore his thinning black hair half way down his back. Long ago he had settled for the slow, contented way of life on Tomango, but only in the last few years had "Mister Harry" become "Mister *Hippy* Harry". It was all the same to him.

The shack was filled with books and shells, fishing rods and piles of old newspapers—and hens. For Hippy Harry kept them, too. Except that *he* allowed them to cluck their way in and out the back door, to flap on to every surface, scratching away happily and unnoticed. Except when there were visitors.

"Come on!" Hippy Harry shouted now, "out you go!"

He swept two hens to the floor from the long wooden table and made room for his bare elbows among the unwashed enamel plates. "Is it raining outside? You two look like orphans of the storm. Never saw such long faces." He gave a huge sigh and cupped his stubbly chin. "All right, let's have the story, boys . . ."

Christopher told him the events of last night—and the morning. Finally, he took the fat gold coin from the pocket of his jeans and laid it down before Hippy Harry.

They all looked at it for a while in awed silence.

At last Hippy Harry uncupped his chin and touched the coin with a finger that was none too clean. "Right! Know what it is? Well, it's a *Spanish doubloon*. Old Spanish money . . . couple of centuries old. Christopher! Picking it up was bad enough, but running away with it . . ." The long hair swished on his back as Hippy Harry shook his head. "That's bad. Very bad!"

"But I was excited. I—I clean forgot all about that part of the story." Christopher couldn't help feeling annoyed that *nobody* understood his shock and delight on the beach. "Even Jonah would have done the same——"

"Not me! This boy's got brains."

"Simmer down, you two. Well, the thing is . . . just how do we frighten them off when they come back to reclaim the doubloon? They'll do it tonight. The moon will still be full."

"We thought they would," Christopher said, gulping.

"He in mortal danger, Mista Harry!" Jonah echoed. Jonah quite liked the phrase. He also liked the look of a bunch of bananas, dangling from a low roof-beam. He tried hard to put the bananas out of his mind. "But I sleep in his room and I don't 'fraid easy. You ask Masta Chris."

"Jonah *is* awfully brave——" Christopher began loyally, but Hippy Harry cried: "I've got it! They all died on the gallows—every black-hearted rogue. You do

93

know that hanging was the punishment for piracy on the high seas, don't you boys?" Hippy Harry slapped an open palm on the pile of old newspapers on the rickety table. His sharp blue eyes swung from one boy's face to the other. "I'm going to rig up a miniature gallows—with cross-arm, dangling noose, and so on. All in bamboo and wood. Then you put the model over your bed, Chris . . . and *they* will take fright instead. It's like showing a crucifix to a vampire. You'll have 'em out of your room before you can say '*pieces of eight*'."

Hippy Harry grinned cheerfully at them both—as his left hand slid the coin smoothly from sight under the pile of old newspapers.

"Well, boys, I must get to work. I'll have your little charm ready in about an hour. What will you two do in the meantime?"

Jonah had the answer.

"We get us a few ripe mangoes!" he said promptly, and Christopher gave him a quick glance to see if he, too, had seen what Hippy Harry had done with the coin. But Jonah's mind was firmly on food. "Ain't it ripe time for guavas, too? How much can we eat, Mista Harry?"

"All you can hold!" And Hippy Harry waved cheerfully, then disappeared into the back room of the shack.

"Glutton!" Christopher said, wandering over to the single window. There was a very fat goat eating the lower leaves of the sunflower trees, and he watched with interest.

But he turned from the window when Jonah said: "Now, boy—no need to get shaky at the knees!" And Christopher laughed, for Jonah was now seated at the rickety table, doing a very good imitation of Hippy Harry. With a hand on the pile of old newspapers, Jonah grinned, then he nodded wisely. "You come to the right place, Christopher. Them ghost pirates are in mortal danger now . . ."

"And how about those sweet, sweet mangoes?" Christopher asked. He knew that the mere mention of fruit would get his friend out of the chair, through the back door, and up the nearest tree.

And it did.

The boys climbed and ate and laughed for more than an hour. They forgot all about the coming night and its possible terrors. Then Hippy Harry called them back out of the bright heat into the cool dimness of the shack.

"Well, boys . . . what do you think of it?"

Christopher and Jonah looked at the model gallows in silence. It looked both crude and toy like and yet, somehow, very real indeed. The thick cord that dangled from the arm of the gallows was pulled into a tight noose. And with his neck in the tight noose was the rigid figure of a pirate.

"The figure came from a toy kit I bought last year. It adds that last finishing touch." Hippy Harry gazed proudly at his handiwork. "It'll do the trick, boys. You'll see. Now, have you got any kind of shelf above your bed, Chris?"

Christopher nodded, his eyes still glued to the frightful model.

"Jonah, is there a big battery torch up at the bungalow?"

It was Jonah's turn to nod.

"Good," said Hippy Harry. "Well, when they come, and Chris here starts yelling—that will be your cue, Jonah. You turn your torch on that shelf and keep it steady. They'll simply melt away at the sight of the gallows. Just take my word for it."

The two boys sighed in unison. Then Jonah said: You can carry my mangoes, Masta Chris. I'll hold that— that *thing* . . ."

Christopher gulped. He suddenly felt very grateful for having a friend as brave as Jonah. They said their goodbyes to hippy Harry and went back out into the blaze of the noonday sun.

They reached the bungalow in the early afternoon and spent the hours till dark trying to avoid Salome. But they couldn't avoid her for ever. At early supper, just before sunset, she said to Christopher: "You hear me,

95

Masta Chris? Why you not eating your fried breadfruit? You always saying you *like* fried breadfruit——"

"He got troubles," Jonah cut in. "But I'll have his piece, Ma, after I finish mine." All the same, Christopher noticed that Jonah, too, was off his food—for once.

"You two keep stuffing your bellies with ripe mangoes . . ." Salome grumbled when she finally took their plates back to the kitchen.

Then the boys sat silent, watching the huge sun stain land and sky a deep crimson, then very slowly drop into the sea without making even a tiny splash. They stayed silent as the tropic night came alive . . . the frogs croaked, the fire-flies winked and glowed, and the mosquitoes came whining out of the star-filled dark.

They sat on, smacking at the mosquitoes, for a while longer.

"We'd better go in," Christopher said reluctantly. "I heard Salome go down to her cottage. I do wish that your mother would sleep in the house. Especially to-night."

"Ma likes her own place, you know that. Anyways, them pirates will be after her gold teeth the moment she opens her mouth to scream."

That made Christopher laugh, but Jonah didn't even smile at his own joke.

"Stop worrying, Jonah," said Christopher. "We'll be all right with the gallows thing. In fact, I don't think that they will come *here* at all." Christopher tried to sound off-hand and mysterious, both at the same time. "They just might call on someone else we know, instead."

But Jonah didn't seem to hear any of it, for he just said: "I sleep in the hammock, eh?"

"Well," Christopher said. "if you'd rather come into my bed . . ."

"With the *thing* over me head?" Jonah grinned then. "No, it's the hammock for me. And the big torch."

They took a long time to fall asleep.

Yet they finally did, lulled by the far-away sound of the sea and the wind in the coconut trees. Then, much later—and very slowly—a huge moon climbed into the night sky, and its light spilt through the wooden shutters of the room where the boys were now soundly sleeping.

And on the stroke of midnight the pirates came.

Suddenly they filled the room, clear and sharp to see, yet ghostly and untouchable as the moonlight. They swore and shouted, banged their pistols on the walls and the wooden shutters, slapped their cutlasses on the foot of Christopher's bed . . .

"Wake up, laddie. The gold!"

"We'll have the coin back . . ."

"Cap'n, slit his thiefin' throat?"

And a moment later, the pirates made way for Captain Skull.

Slowly he advanced on Christopher until his fleshless head was just inches away and the empty eye-sockets were two deep pools of evil. The lower jaw swung down as the Captain made ready to speak.

It was too much for Christopher. "I haven't got it," he wailed. "I haven't got the coin! Jonah! *The torch* . . ."

From the madly swinging hammock came a sudden beam of light. It went clean through the pirates like a bright sword blade—and straight into Christopher's eyes.

"On the shelf, Jonah! *The shelf* . . ."

But now the hammock was swinging more violently than ever. Then Jonah fell out of the hammock and hit the wooden floor with a thud, and the torch rolled away, spilling a line of brilliant light.

His jaws clinking and clattering, Captain Skull roared: "It's the little blackamoor! He has the doubloon!" The Captain had turned away from Christopher, and now the eye-less sockets and one skeleton hand were all pointing squarely at Jonah.

The pirates had gone silent for a moment, but now they again erupted into shouted oaths and threats.

"I'll have your liver for breakfast!"

"Give the gold over . . ."

"You'll walk the plank!"

Jonah came shakily to his feet, then he threw something high into the roof. "Take it then." Jonah shouted, half sobbing. "I wanted the gold for me ma. I never give her anything before!"

A dozen unwashed faces were upturned, a dozen pairs of red-rimmed eyes watched the coin spin in the moonlight . . . then a huge skeleton hand shot up and caught it in mid-air. And at that exact moment, Captain Skull and his pirates vanished. In a split second the room held only the moonlight and the two shaking boys.

In the sudden silence, Jonah swallowed the other half of his sob.

"Jonah . . . ?" Christopher shook his head in bewilderment. "How did you get the coin? I *saw* Hippy Harry steal it!"

"Me, too." Jonah came over to the bed and took a deep breath. "So I sit in his chair, then I take the coin from under the papers. Sorry, Masta Chris . . . but you know how my ma likes gold on she teeth. It was gonna be a present, see?"

"Well, they got it back," Christopher said, sighing with relief. "Put on the light, Jonah."

"What for?"

Christopher grinned in the moonlight. "Now that I'm no longer in mortal danger . . . I feel mortal hungry! Don't *you*?"

"You bet!" Jonah said, brightening. "You stay in bed . . . I'll go hunting. I know just where Ma hid some fried chicken—from me!"

Christopher was laughing when he reached up for Hippy Harry's 'charm', still dangling over his head. Then he threw the model of gallows and pirates right across the room.

By then Jonah had vanished.

Jonah believed in speed when the object was food.

GOODBYE, CHARLOTTE

by MARGARET BIGGS

RACHEL liked the new house. It was much bigger than their old one, where you could hear what everybody was saying in every room. She had a bedroom of her own, too, no longer having to share with Toby, and from its wide window-seat she could see past the bent, twisted oak tree to the old rose-brick wall at the bottom of the overgrown garden. She loved it all. She could cycle to school easily from here, instead of having the long, boring bus journey. Toby liked it all too, she knew, and Tabs, the retriever, bounded gaily and wildly up and down stairs, getting his bearings and revelling in the extra space.

But it was miserable with her mother still in hospital, and nobody knowing when she would come home. A shadow lay across everything. Home wasn't home, Rachel thought, without Mum humming as she peeled potatoes, or sitting cross-legged on the low couch, struggling with the crossword. Toby felt the same, she knew, though he never said so. He hated grumblers.

It had been appendicitis, sudden and agonising and out of the blue, that had sent Mrs. Wimbush into hospital in the middle of the night, just after they had moved here. And then she had run a temperature after the operation, and was still recovering far too slowly, and Mr. Wimbush looked wan and shadowed under the eyes when he came back each night from the hospital.

"Dad, she *is* getting better, isn't she?" Rachel asked, bravely putting her fears into words, one night when he got home, four days after the operation.

Her father looked at her and slowly nodded, passing a weary hand across his forehead. "Yes, thank God, but it was touch and go. Complications—well, I can't go into it all, but the sister tells me she can't be discharged for at least another week. She's had to have a blood transfusion, you know, Rachel, and they've got her in a side ward for extra peace and quiet. But she looked better tonight, and sent you and Toby her love, and wants you to go and visit her at the weekend. I gave her your letter, and she's going to write back."

"Oh good. It's so horrid with her not here," said Rachel vehemently.

Her father forced a smile and squeezed her hand. "I know. But we'll manage for a few more days. You and Toby can cope, can't you?"

"Of course we can." Rachel rose to the occasion, feeling he needed cheering up as much as she did. "You know that—though I have to hound Toby to do his share of the washing-up!"

But it was lonely, especially when they got home from school. Toby had the habit of departing upstairs to his hi-fi, and listening, deaf and blind to the rest of the world. Rachel, used to telling her mother what had been going on at school all day, felt left out. She would make herself a sandwich, thickly plastered with peanut butter, and wander about. She took to sitting on her window-seat, staring out. She liked the shapes of the trees. Through them she could just see the three other new houses, but they were all set well apart, and far back from the road. She gathered there had been a rambling old house here, which the builders had demolished, and each new house had a quarter of the old grounds. It was uncannily quiet here, away from the constant noise of traffic on the main road past their old house. Rachel honestly liked it—yet there was something lonely in the air, which she felt as soon as she came in. Or was it simply because Mum was in hospital, and her best friend, Jenny, was now too far away to visit after school? No, there was a certain indescribable feel about the house, a kind of melancholy.

"Do you notice anything about this house? A sort of sad feeling?" she was driven to ask Toby one day, as they sat at tea-time eating baked beans on toast (the toast rather burnt, as Toby was not slow to point out).

Toby stared at her a minute, his mouth open for the

next bite. Then he grinned and said: "You're a bit loopy sometimes," in his specially detached voice. He began to talk about football—but Rachel was sure he knew what she meant, though he refused to admit it. Toby was always sternly practical.

That night her father came back from the hospital very glum. Her mother was no better, very weak, and hadn't eaten anything all day. Rachel felt very sad. She made her father have some hot soup, and tried to get him to have an omelette, but he said he had eaten already. Rachel didn't believe him. She could see by his face how upset he was. She went up to bed and read for a long time, but when she put the light off she couldn't go to sleep. The more she tried, the more impossible it was. She kept thinking about her mother. What if she—but no, she mustn't think that. Rachel blinked hard, forcing the tears to stay unshed. It would be babyish to cry. But it was so wretched not to be able to *do* anything to help! That was the worst of it. At long last Rachel drifted off into an uneasy sleep, still anxious and apprehensive.

She awoke with a start. The room was still dark, and she guessed it must be the middle of the night, but somewhere very near someone was crying—quietly, desperately. It wasn't Toby or her father—it sounded like a girl. But who? Rachel sat up and said bravely into the darkness: "Who's there? What's the matter?"

There was a terrified gulp, and then a girl's voice said shakily: "It's I—Charlotte. Who is that?"

Rachel clicked on her bedside lamp. In its dim light she saw a girl of about her own age, in a long white cotton nightdress with lace around the neck, and an old-fashioned-looking pink wrapper on top. The girl had a thin, pale face, and dark, wavy hair, loose to her waist. In one thin hand she clutched a sodden handkerchief.

They stared at each other. Rachel thought: This is mad. I must be still dreaming. "What's the matter?" she said again, not frightened but mystified.

The girl stood quite still at the foot of her bed. "I—I don't know who you are. I can't understand . . . I couldn't sleep because I'm so worried about Mamma."

101

"Mamma?" repeated Rachel questioningly. The unfamiliar word startled her. "Your mother, do you mean?"

"Yes. She's very ill at home. I know, because Papa wrote and told me. I do so much want to go home and help look after her, but Miss March reads all our letters, and she—she says I must not tell Mamma how unhappy I am, and that I must stay here until the end of the term, and not be a nuisance. But that will be weeks, and I know Mamma wants me at home—I have nursed her before." Charlotte wiped her face with her handkerchief, and gazed despairingly at Rachel. "I am not being selfish, am I? I know I really could help. And Papa is so worried . . ." She added: "I hate it here."

"Where is here?" demanded Rachel, intrigued.

Charlotte looked at her in puzzled fashion. "Here at Miss March's school, of course. She is so very strict, and she makes us all write letters home saying how happy we are—but we aren't! The rooms are so cold, and we often feel hungry. But I could put up with it if only Mamma were well. But she has not been strong for months, and Papa writes she has got worse since I left home. He didn't want to send me, but my aunt persuaded him it was best. He is vicar of Cheveley."

Rachel recognised the name. It was a pretty village, a tourist spot fifteen miles the other side of town. She had had tea there once, at a tea-room called The Bubbling Kettle her mother had taken a fancy to.

"This isn't a school," she said gently. "It's a house, and I live here."

Charlotte wrinkled her brow. "I know that it is a house —it is called Denning House. But it is Miss March's school for girls. You must be one of us. There are thirty of us here." She stared wonderingly at Rachel, and shivered.

"Come into bed a minute. You look frozen," suggested Rachel.

Charlotte slipped in docilely beside her. She was obviously used to doing what she was told. Rachel felt protective towards her. She seemed so helpless.

"This road is called Denning Close," she observed thoughtfully. As she spoke, she suddenly remembered the old house, pulled down and vanished. Had *that* been Denning House?

Charlotte did not answer, too absorbed in her thoughts. At last she said: "I wish I understood. Either this must be a dream, or—are you one of the maids? Or have you just arrived at the school?"

"I go to a comprehensive in Selbury," said Rachel. "It's a—a different sort of school." Suddenly she had an idea. "Charlotte, what year is it?"

After a pause Charlotte said in bewilderment: "It is 1890, of course. Had you forgotten?"

It was Rachel's turn to shiver. But before she could answer, Charlotte went on quickly: "I must go. If Miss March finds me in here with you, I shall be in dire disgrace. But if only I could write home properly, without her seeing the letter!"

"Write secretly, and don't let the old beast see. You can slip out and post it, can't you? Then your father will probably come to take you home," suggested Rachel.

"Oh, if only I could—but it would be impossible. We are never allowed out on our own." Charlotte was gazing at her, a gleam of hope in her intense, dark eyes.

"It's worth a try," said Rachel sleepily. Suddenly, strangely, she could hardly keep her eyes open. "Do try, Charlotte. Don't give up!"

Charlotte nodded. "I will. Thank you—I don't even know your name, but you are *very* kind!"

"I'm Rachel." And then, what seemed only a few seconds later, Rachel found herself waking up in the cold, wintry, morning light, with the first thrushes calling across the grass from the oak tree.

"What a weird dream," she thought, stretching. It still seemed uncannily vivid, and Charlotte's thin, tear-stained face lingered in her memory.

"Dad," she said at breakfast, as they hurriedly crunched cornflakes, "did you ever see the old house that was here before the builders pulled it down in the autumn?"

Her father stared in surprise, and put down his spoon. "What on earth made you think of that?"

Toby, too, directed a searching glance at her.

"I'm just interested," Rachel said defensively.

"Let me think," said Mr. Wimbush. He drank some coffee. "Yes, that's right—when your mother and I drove over the first time it was still standing. They were knocking down the stables. Very old-fashioned it was, of course—red brick. Early Victorian, I should imagine. Huge sash windows. Yes, now I come to think of it, our house is built pretty well exactly where the middle section stood. The brick wall down the garden is part of the original wall, of course—they left what was of any use."

"Was it called Denning House?" asked Rachel casually.

"That's right." Her father smiled faintly. "You going to write up some local history?"

"I might," said Rachel, and jumped up as she heard the time on Toby's transistor. "Heavens, I must dash. I'll get the bread on the way home, Dad."

That night, after a long and hectic day, she felt happier when she got into bed. Her mother had been better that evening, and Mr. Wimbush had come back hugely relieved. He even brought two letters for Rachel and Toby. Their mother's writing was stronger, less wobbly. Rachel felt tired but much more relaxed. As she drifted off to sleep, Charlotte came into her thoughts, for the first time since breakfast. A strange coincidence, that both her mother and Charlotte's should be ill. It was a jumble, and Rachel couldn't work it all out. She was too tired to think any more, and fell asleep instantly.

She awoke with a jump, to hear someone calling her name, low but clear. "Rachel—oh, Rachel, can you hear me? Please, Rachel . . ." Floating out of deep sleep, Rachel knew instantly it was Charlotte, and felt glad.

"I'm here, Charlotte. Tell me, did you post the letter?"

In the darkness, a dim shape stood beside her bed. "Oh, Rachel, I was trying to find you. It was dreadful. Miss March caught me going down the drive with the

104

letter in my pocket, just as I got to the oak tree—you know the one? She was furious, because I was out alone, and sent me up to the dormitory without supper. I didn't mind *that*, but the letter is still in my pocket—I dared not tell her about it, of course—and she will be watching me now, so I fear I shall never get it posted!"

"What a blight she is," said Rachel sympathetically.

"A—a blight?" The word seemed new to Charlotte.

"A horror. A tyrant," said Rachel, not mincing her words.

"Oh yes, she *is* a tyrant," Charlotte agreed. "We all think that. Even her sisters are scared of her. She boxed my ears. But I would not let her see me cry," she added.

"Jolly good," said Rachel. "You're about twelve like me, aren't you?"

"Yes. I have two little brothers at home, Edward and Charles." Charlotte sighed. "I know I could help them all greatly if I got home again. Papa misses me, I know, and only sent me because he felt he ought, for my sake. I'm sure it is costing him more than he can afford. That is why Miss March wants me to stay. She wants to save a lot of money and then go abroad, Louisa told me. Louisa has been here three years, poor thing, and hates it just as much as I do!"

"It's a pity you can't all go home, and she'd have to close down her rotten old school," said Rachel indignantly. "Look, you said there were some maids—couldn't one of them post the letter for you?"

"I only talk to one maid, who helps us with our hair. She is the same age as I am. I wonder if I could ask her?" Charlotte sounded doubtful. "I would hate to get her into trouble. Miss March would discharge her if she found out, and her family are very poor, I know. She lives in the village, and goes home every night."

"If you can trust her, I should try her," urged Rachel. She felt as keenly as Charlotte that the letter must be posted. "I know how you feel, because my mother's ill, too," she found herself adding.

"Oh, Rachel, I'm so sorry!" Charlotte sounded very concerned. "I'm so full of my troubles, and you have

105

plenty of your own. Papa would call me selfish, and so I am."

"No, you're not, not a scrap," said Rachel. She reached out and tried to squeeze Charlotte's fingers, but her own slipped through them.

"Why did you ask me what year it is?" asked Charlotte wonderingly. "I was thinking about that all day."

Rachel found it impossible to explain. "Never mind that." She tried a brisk tone. "Cheer up—I'm sure you'll get away from that horrid place soon."

Charlotte's pale face beamed at her. "If I do, Rachel, it will be because of you. Isn't it strange—I seem to find you whenever I feel particularly sad? I can't understand how, though—and this room is so unlike all the others." She gazed round at Rachel's bedroom, puzzled.

"I can't understand either, but it doesn't matter." Suddenly the heavy, compelling sleepiness was coming over Rachel again. "It's no good, I can't stay awake," she muttered. "Goodnight, Charlotte. I'll be thinking of you."

"And I, you, Rachel. Goodnight. I think I shall be able to go to sleep now. And I do hope your mamma will be well soon!"

In Rachel's ears, Charlotte's voice was floating far away, the words distorting and turning into gibberish as she fell asleep.

That afternoon, after school, Rachel went purposefully to the public library in Selbury, and searched through the reference section. Digging among old, faintly musty local history volumes, she at last came across one specifically dealing with Selbury and the area around. Turning the pages quickly on and on, she stopped dead. There was a large water-colour of the old house, exactly as her father had described it. There it stood, large, imposing, with tall chimneys. And to one side stood the gnarled oak tree, exactly as it looked today. Rachel recognised it with a leap of the heart. At the foot of the sketch was written in flowing, curling letters: "Denning House. Miss Victoria March's residence, and a highly reputed school for young ladies. 1889."

Rachel gazed and gazed, her head whirling. It was all true! She sat in a trance, oblivious of the bustle of the busy library round her. How had she and Charlotte come into this strange contact? It was unbelievable, but it had happened—and here *she* sat, over eighty years later.

"Charlotte must be dead," she thought, and hated the thought. "But *then*, when she was my age, and was worried about her mother, just like me, somehow we got on each other's wavelength. I was on the same spot, all these years later, and miserable, just where she was miserable, long ago."

At last she carefully replaced the book on the shelf, and walked slowly out to her bicycle. She felt dazed, and it would not have surprised her to see carriages and horses on the main road, instead of the endless, noisy stream of cars and lorries.

That night her father came home early, bringing delicious fish and chips, and while they ate he told them jubilantly that the hospital had rung him up at the office. "Your mother's doing so well, she can definitely come home next Monday, so long as her temperature stays down. Isn't that great?" He looked happier than for weeks.

"Great," Toby agreed, and dug Rachel in the ribs. "Isn't it?"

"Oh—yes, absolutely perfect," said Rachel fervently. It was, of course. But as she went on eating fish and chips, she kept thinking, "What about Charlotte's mother? Will she be all right?"

She hoped Charlotte would come again that night— but nothing happened, nor the next, nor the night after. Rachel was disappointed and concerned. Of course, it had all happened already, but somehow it still seemed to be happening now. At the week-end, all the time she was tidying up the house, helping get things presentable for her mother's return, she kept thinking and brooding about Charlotte. Perhaps her mother had died, and she had never got home—no, surely not! It was so awful not to

107

know, like reading a book and finding the last chapter torn out. Charlotte had been so vulnerable, so urgently in need of help. "It must have been a lousy school," thought Rachel with feeling.

On Sunday night she went to sleep happily, thinking: "Mum will be home tomorrow. I'll do her a special tea." It was a lovely, warming thought. But still interweaved with that was her concern for Charlotte.

This time she didn't wake up, but she began to dream. It was sharp and vivid, like watching a film in a small frame. She could see Charlotte in a gloomy, dark-looking room, hurriedly packing a small trunk. She looked flustered and anxious. Rachel tried to speak to her, but this time she could not get through. She could only watch. It seemed to be evening—a candle was flickering. Suddenly the door of the room swung open, and a formidable-looking woman swept in. "Miss March," realised Rachel. Miss March was speaking angrily, making wide gestures. "Telling her off," thought Rachel indignantly. She ended by pointing to the trunk imperiously. Charlotte crammed the last garments inside, and knelt to shut it. Miss March stood waiting impatiently as she pulled on a long, dark coat. Then, leaving the trunk on the floor, presumably for one of the servants to carry downstairs, she seized Charlotte's arm and led her out. The empty room faded. The scene was over.

Rachel woke at the usual time, and lay thinking. Charlotte was going, but she had not looked happy—anything but. What had happened? Had Miss March intercepted the letter, and sent her home in disgrace? That seemed unlikely, from what Charlotte had said. Had a message come that her mother was worse? That seemed more probable, from Charlotte's face. "I don't wonder she hated Miss March—I wouldn't have liked to have stood up to her myself," thought Rachel. "She looked tough as an old boot!"

But then Toby came pounding at her door, shouting to her to get a move on, couldn't she? Had she forgotten Mum was coming home today, and there was still stacks to be done? And Rachel jumped up, shouting: "I'll be

A formidable-looking woman swept in . . .

down in five minutes—don't fuss!" and had no time to think any more about Charlotte.

The following week was busy but immensely satisfying. Mrs. Wimbush came home, looking fragile but gloriously happy. When Rachel got back and burst through the back door, shouting: "Mum—Mum—are you really here?" her mother got up from the kitchen table, where she had been sitting, and opened her arms with a beaming smile. "Oh, darling—but hug me gently, Rachel—oh, this is so lovely!" And Rachel, hugging her as instructed, felt properly herself again, complete, as she had not felt for weeks.

"We'll wait on you hand and foot," she promised her mother exuberantly.

"Will you?" said her mother, smiling, between laughter and tears. "Well, I feel very proud of myself—I've just made my first pot of tea, so sit down and tell me what you think of it. And, more important, what you've been doing all this time?"

"She's been mooning about, mainly," said Toby, perched on the refrigerator, swinging his legs. But he too looked wildly happy, though he tried to conceal the fact.

Yes, it was lovely and glorious, having Mum back, but despite all the talking and laughing and gossiping, Rachel could not forget about Charlotte. The feeling of loneliness that had hung over the house vanished, but somehow Rachel still felt a scrap lonely, inside. She still possessed the deep concern about Charlotte, and she still desperately wanted to know the end of the story. How could she rejoice in her own mother being back, when she was still in uncertainty about Charlotte's? It was so selfish and unfair of her. Though outwardly the family settled back into their old routine, Rachel went on turning the same thought over and over in her mind. Had Charlotte's story ended happily, or not?

"Anything the matter, love?" said her mother one evening, looking anxiously at her. "You've been staring into space for ages."

Rachel jumped guiltily. "Oh no—don't worry, Mum,

it's nothing!" And she hastily switched on the television, to prevent further questions.

"Something on your mind, Rachel?" said her father next morning, as she was zipping up her anorak in the hall. "You're so quiet."

"I haven't got to keep talking all the time, Dad, have I?" said Rachel, flushing.

Her father looked intently at her. "Of course not. So long as you're not worrying about anything."

"No, honestly I'm not— I must get my bike and rush, Dad, I'm late already. See you tonight!" And Rachel darted off to escape.

"I must forget all about Charlotte—if I can," she thought, as she cycled to school. "I can't seem to dream about her now. It's over, so I've got to forget her. But I *do* wish I knew!"

No more dreams came, and Rachel continued, despite all her efforts, to worry. "Of course I shan't dream about her again—it can't happen, because she left Denning House that last time," she thought forlornly. It was like having an aching tooth—however hard she tried, she couldn't put it out of her mind.

"What's up with you?" said Toby, meeting her outside the house on their way home that afternoon. He stared, half critical, half concerned. Girls were a closed book to him, but he had a soft spot for his sister, and he could see there was *something* . . .

"Oh, nothing. Why does everyone keep bothering me?" flared Rachel, losing her temper in a manner unusual to her.

"All right, sorry I spoke," said Toby, shrugging. "But I wish you'd get over whatever you're bothered about, because Mum's worrying, I know, and you don't want that, do you?"

Rachel felt guiltier than ever as she hurried to put her bicycle into the garage. She felt she was in a maze and couldn't find the way out. It was a panicky feeling.

At the weekend her mother could go out for a drive. Spring was coming now, though it was still cold. Mr. Wimbush said: "Let's all go out to see the country, and maybe the first lambs. It would cheer us all up." He glanced at Rachel as he spoke, but she avoided his eye.

"Oh, that would be lovely," said Mrs. Wimbush happily. "I've been shut off from the outside world so much, lately. Bless you, Ken!"

"Wrap up warm then, love. And if you feel like it, we'll have tea out," promised Mr. Wimbush.

So off they went, with Rachel and Toby in the back, and Mrs. Wimbush, a rug around her legs, despite her protests, gazing with delight out at the countryside. They got off the main roads and into the lanes, and Rachel leaned forward against her mother's shoulders, while Mrs. Wimbush kept up a running commentary. "Oh, just look at those catkins—aren't they beautiful? . . . Can you stop here a minute, Ken? I must look at those lambs, they can't be more than a week old, and out in this wind, poor little things! Look, Toby, did you see those pheasants in the field, near that barn?" She was bubbling over with excitement, and Rachel felt indulgent. Dear Mum, it was because of her they had moved out further into the country. There was nothing she enjoyed more than this sort of trip, or a long, muddy walk over the windswept fields.

"Well, how about this for tea, this place here?" said Mr. Wimbush eventually, pulling up outside a long, low house. "We came to it once before, and you liked it."

"I remember—what a good idea. Yes, there's the sign up there, with the kettle steaming and bubbling away on it," Mrs. Wimbush answered.

Rachel gave herself a little shake, and looked round. A church, grey, with a low tower and a creaking weather-vane, stood across the triangular green. Pink- and white-washed cottages were grouped along one side of the green, and a small brook wound beside the lane. It was Cheveley. Rachel took a deep breath as a sudden idea hit her.

"I want to look round the churchyard. I'll only be a few minutes. Can I catch you up in the tea-room, then?"

"Of course, darling, if you like," said her mother, struggling to unwind the rug.

"Rachel's writing a book about this part of the world, you know," her father joked. And Toby blew a raspberry.

Rachel escaped her family and ran across the green, and in under the lych-gate to the churchyard. Her heart was thumping, and she had the feeling that something—she didn't know what—was about to be revealed.

If only I knew her surname, she thought. But I know her first name, and her brothers' names, and that ought to be enough.

She scurried about among the older tombstones, scanning each, then hurrying on. The grass scratched her legs. Was it hopeless? But something was telling her to go on. And suddenly she came upon what she was looking for, as if it had been waiting for her. A tall stone, with the black lettering half-covered in lichen, standing near the church porch. Rachel knelt beside it and read.

"Augusta Wade, wife of the Rev. William Wade, Vicar of this parish. Mother of Charlotte, Edward, and Charles. B. 1857, d. 1925. Deeply mourned by her husband and children. Well done, thou good and faithful servant."

Rachel wanted to skip and dance. "So she *did* get better," she thought triumphantly. "She did! Charlotte must have got the letter posted, and her father came to fetch her, and she helped nurse her mother, just as she wanted to. And it was all right!"

She knelt there, staring at the stone, while the long grass around her moved and whispered in the cold wind, and above her the weather-vane creaked. Then at last, slowly, reluctantly, she stood up.

"Goodbye, Charlotte," she said aloud, and walked out of the churchyard, closing the gate carefully behind her.

THE VACKIE

by MARY DANBY

"HOLIDAY work," announced Mr. Lawler. "I want you to write a composition about where you live—your house, or your flat." He picked up a piece of chalk. "MY HOME," he wrote on the blackboard.

"What if you live in a caravan?" asked a girl by the window.

"Write about that." The teacher brushed chalk from his hands, impatient to end the lesson.

The boy at the desk next to John Rogers grimaced. "Why couldn't it be 'A Day in the Life of a Footballer', or 'How I Would Survive on Mars'?" he grumbled.

John smiled in sympathy. The small, end-of-terrace house where he lived with his parents and sister was so ordinary that it could be adequately described in half a dozen lines. He would have to make his writing extra-large to cover the paper. "My Home." How dreary could you get?

"No more questions? Right, let's be off," said Mr. Lawler.

"My Home," John wrote at the top of a clean page as, two weeks later, he lay on his bedroom floor confronting his exercise book. He sighed, then slowly underlined the words.

"My home is 15 Maybury Crescent. It is a tall, thin house made of greyish-brown bricks with houses just the same all down the road. It has a green front door.

Bored already with his composition, he went downstairs and turned on the television. His sister Jean came in with her hair in curlers and, without asking, changed channels.

"Hey!" said John, but decided not to make a fight

of it. None of the programmes seemed worth watching, anyway.

He wandered into the kitchen to see if tea was ready. It wasn't. His mother was busy washing clothes and turned from the sink to ask: "What were you up to in this shirt? There's oil all over the cuffs."

"My bike," said John, backing out of the room before she could tell him off. He might as well go and finish that wretched composition, then he wouldn't have to bother with it for the rest of the holidays.

Upstairs, he sat on his bed, reading what he had already written.

"... *It is a tall, thin house ... It has a red front door.*"

A red front door? That wasn't right. It had a *green* front door. Funny. He couldn't have been concentrating when he wrote it. Not surprising, when they gave you such boring subjects to write about. Now he'd have to cross out "red" and write "green", and maybe lose a mark for untidiness. But then, Mr. Lawler had never been to the house, so how would he know "red" was wrong? Perhaps it was best to leave it.

"*There are three bedrooms, a bathroom, a lounge and a kitchen,*" he continued. "*The kitchen is dark because there is a tree outside the window. The sink is on the left.*"

John chewed the end of his pen, then studied the pattern on the bedspread. There was a fly crawling along the edge of his bedside table, and John put a coin and a pencil in front of it, to make an obstacle course, but the fly worked its way around them.

"*My bedroom is nearly square. It has a big window facing the door.*"

John counted the lines he had written so far. Only nine. Mr. Lawler would want at least twenty-four. What else could he say?

"*We came to Newbury in 1977, because my father got a job here. It is quite nice. The house is like the one in London, but here there are fields quite near and it is quieter.*"

"John!" His mother was calling him. "John! Stephen's here and wants to know if you're going to the shops with him. You could get me a loaf of bread for tea."

So the composition was once again put aside, and John, in his rush to join his friend downstairs, accidentally kicked the exercise book under his bed.

It stayed there until a week later, when John went into his room and found his mother standing by the window, reading his composition.

"Oh," he said despondently, remembering the ten more lines he still had to cover.

She handed him the book. "*I* don't know," she said, smiling as she gathered up a pile of dirty sheets. "Your imagination!"

"Eh?" John couldn't see how anyone could describe the composition as imaginative. Deadly, more like. He began to read it through again, searching his words for signs of literary genius.

His words? No, not these. His writing, most definitely, but *someone else's words.*

"We came to Newbury in 1939, because of the air raids on London. They called us 'vackies', which meant evacuees—the children who were moved to safe places in the country. Our parents stayed behind, because of Dad's job at the munitions factory."

Air raids? Munitions? John couldn't have written all that, not even at his most absent-minded. He didn't know what munitions were. Guns, was it? Yet it was certainly his own, rather untidy handwriting.

His heart began to beat unnaturally fast, and he lay back on the bed and closed his eyes. His head felt loose, somehow, as if it might at any moment come adrift and roll to the floor. When he opened his eyes, the room seemed darker than usual, although the sun outside was as summer-holiday bright as he'd ever seen it. He sat up slowly and reached for the exercise book.

"My name is Leonard Thompson. Back home my name was always Tommy, only here I'm called Leonard, which my sister Edna says sounds like someone posh. 'Lee-o-nard,' she goes, when she wants to annoy me. But

116

I'd rather be Tommy, and I'd rather live in Hackney, like we did before."

The writing danced before John's eyes, making him dizzy, but he read on.

"When Mrs. Gedge first saw us, Edna and me, she said: 'Ah, my two little visitors,' and we thought she looked ever so kind and jolly. We had jam for tea, and we hadn't had jam for simply ages."

That was all there was. An unpleasant chill enveloped John as he stared at these strange sentences, written apparently by him, and yet not by him.

Suddenly he pushed the exercise book away from him, as if it were alive and menacing. "No!" he said out loud. "No!"

"What's that, dear?" said his mother, armed with fresh sheets from the airing cupboard. "Something the matter?"

John wanted to tell her what had happened, but he found himself saying: "I don't feel well. I want to go to sleep."

The thermometer was fetched, but there were no signs of fever. John was declared to be merely "under the weather", which he found irritating. How could you be "over the weather" unless you were in an aeroplane? When he voiced his thought to his mother, she finished making up his bed and said: "If you're going to be silly, you can be silly on your own," then left the room.

He wished she hadn't gone. The room was dark again and horribly quiet. Quiet? Outside the window, at the end of the garden, was a large building site, which normally rang with the clangour of scaffolding poles and the grind of lorries. Something told John not to turn his head, not to look out of that window, in case he should see grass and trees instead of concrete and pulleys.

He returned to the book, half wanting, half dreading to read the rest of the story. For there must be more. He knew that whoever or whatever was playing tricks on him hadn't finished yet.

"After tea, Mrs. Gedge put our clothes away in a cup-

117

board. I was careful not to show her Mum's diamond ring. Mum said to keep it hidden and safe, and I had it tied on a string round my neck, under my shirt.

John's hand went to his chest, in what seemed a familiar movement, patting to make sure that something was secure. Only there was nothing there. Again he felt an icy chill, and slipped deeper under the covers. He looked around the room, in case there was something to see, some visible manifestation of the force that had rewritten his words. At the same time, though, he knew that he was quite alone. In fact, his sense of loneliness was such that he could have been the only person on earth, alone in a desert of grey-brick houses, with only the book in his hand for company.

"We were wrong about Mrs. Gedge. After that first day she wasn't jolly any more—or kind. She only seems like that when people come to call. She takes our things. Edna had a pen and pencil set which Mum and Dad gave her once when they came to visit us. The next week she couldn't find it. Then we saw Mrs. Gedge using the pen, and she said she'd bought it at the corner stationer's. We believed her then, but later I lost my scout knife —it just vanished—and then some of our clothes disappeared. She said we'd grown out of them, but we hadn't. I think she sold them to the second-hand shop.

"And she makes us work all the time. Edna has to clean the house, do the laundry, wash dishes, peel potatoes —oh, everything. And I have to chop wood and carry in the coal, lay the fire, polish the brass and clean out the drains. One day she made me put my arm down a drain, right up past the elbow, and pull out a whole lot of stinking muck. I would have thrown it in her face, only she would have invented something even worse for me. She tells her friends she loves children. All I can say is, what can it be like if she hates you?"

John looked up as his mother came to the door to check on him.

"All right, dear?"

John nodded, unable to move his eyes from the page, and she went away again.

A face appeared behind the paper, so that he couldn't see it clearly, but he knew he was no longer alone. Mrs. Gedge was with him now, and he could see the steeliness in her smile as she handed him a broom. "Every nook and cranny, now, Leonard. You have to earn your keep, you know." She always said that. How did he know? John blinked the image away and returned to the words, his words—whose words?

"Tommy? Tommy Thompson?"

Someone was looking for him, calling to him from a long way off.

"My name is John Rogers, John Derek Rogers," he murmured to himself. "I am not Tommy Thompson, or Leonard, or anyone else."

"Thompson? Thompson?" echoed the voice.

There were more words on the paper.

"I wrote to Mum and Dad and asked them to fetch us home. We wouldn't mind the bombs, we said. But the letter came back, unopened, and a man in a grey mackintosh was at the door, asking to see Mrs. Gedge. He sat with her for ages, talking and talking, while Edna and I played cards in the kitchen. When he went, she came quietly to us and sat with us at the table. She said there had been an air raid, that Mum and Dad hadn't reached the shelter in time. Edna cried, and Mrs. Gedge pulled her on to her knee and cuddled her. She told me I could cry, too, as if she thought I ought to, but I didn't, not then."

John felt tears pricking his eyes and sniffed them back. He wouldn't show her, wouldn't let her see the pain that welled up in him, making him swallow convulsively, again and again.

"Mrs. Gedge said we weren't to worry, that she would take care of us, but I had a better idea. I said we'd go to Auntie Joan's. I didn't know where Auntie Joan lived —except that it was somewhere near London—but I was sure we'd find her somehow. Mrs. Gedge said how did we know Auntie Joan would want us? I think she aims to keep us so that we can do her cleaning and run her errands. She's already teaching Edna to cook. In a

couple of years' time she'll have us doing everything for her.

"I've made a plan. I found a loose brick in the floor of the outhouse, and I've put my mother's ring in a tin box and hidden it there. The ring is worth at least fifty pounds, Mum said. She told me I could sell it if ever there was a real emergency.

"Fifty pounds will be more than enough for the fare to London, and any food we need on the way. We'll run away from Maybury Crescent and find Auntie Joan."

John felt suddenly very tired. He closed the book and turned over on his side. But he couldn't sleep. Pictures came, like memories, to flood his brain. A girl in grey stockings, about his own age, with large, round eyes and a fuzz of hair tied back with a ribbon. "Edna," he said softly, and the girl smiled. He saw a man and a woman, their faces blackened and scarred, beckoning to him across a field of flames, and he was running to them. The flames fell away before his feet and sprang up again behind him, so that he could go only forward.

"I'm coming," he muttered, and then everything was a velvet blackness.

"A touch of 'flu, I think," said his father, feeling John's forehead. "There's a lot of it about."

John felt very weak, as if he had been pulling himself up from some deep, dark place. But the room was light again, and warm, and all he could see were the familiar furnishings of his bedroom and the comforting form of his father, now busily straightening the bedclothes and drawing back the curtains. From outside came the clank of scaffolding and the whistle that announced the builders' tea break.

Jean brought him milk and biscuits and sat on the end of the bed. She didn't usually pay much attention to him, and now they were alone together there didn't seem a great deal to say.

"You all right, then?" she asked.

He nodded. Could he tell her what had happened? Should he show her the book, tell her how he had felt,

120

how he had almost *been* this strange boy from nearly forty years ago?

"I say, Jean——" he began, but at the same moment she made some comment about his untidy room, and the moment was lost.

"I say, Mum," he tried later, when he was up and dressed, surprisingly fit-looking after his "touch of 'flu". "Have we got an outhouse?"

She looked up from her magazine. "What do you mean, 'have we got an outhouse'? We've got a garden shed, but I don't know that I'd call it an outhouse. Anyway, you know perfectly well what we've got and haven't got. Really!"

John pretended to be fiddling with something on the sideboard, then, when his mother was once more engrossed in knitting patterns, he slipped through the kitchen and out by the back door.

The shed was full of garden tools and flower pots, and he had to move most of them before he could see the floor properly. One by one, he lifted the loose bricks, but he could find only earth underneath. Then, towards the back, he saw a brick that sat a little higher than the others.

"John!" His mother was at the kitchen window. "What do you think you're up to in there?"

"Nothing, Mum." He quickly lifted the brick and pocketed the small tin box that lay in a hollow beneath it. "Just looking for a piece of string."

Up in his room, he took the box from his pocket and, brushing away the earth that clung to it, he carefully removed the lid.

The box was empty.

There was a sudden high peal of laughter, and he turned round, expecting to see his sister at the door, but there was no one there.

"Leonard and Edna? Yes, I remember them," said an old lady three doors down the street. "Mrs. Gedge's evacuees. I remember *she* was very quiet and polite, but *he*—now, he was a little scamp, always in trouble for

121

this and that. Mrs. Gedge had a hard time with him. They were orphans, you know. Parents died in the Blitz."

"What happened to them?" asked John.

"Ah, now, that was sad," said the old lady, shaking her head. "Young Leonard got run over, you know, just like they always said he would. Never would look before he crossed the road. Used to play 'Last Across' with his pals after school. Died before the ambulance could get to him, poor lad. Of course, little Edna was miserable. But she got over it in time, and she stayed here till she got a cook's job over at Thatcham. Probably married by now. I seem to remember she was walking out with a young man named Caldicott. His parents had the draper's shop in Bartholomew Street."

"Caldicott, Caldicott, Caldicott." John stood in a phone box, scanning the local directory. There were two Caldicotts in Newbury, with the initials E.N. and R.H. He would try the nearest first.

R. H. Caldicott lived in the third of a row of modern semi-detached houses near the railway station. John pressed the bell and heard a cheerful ding-dong echo through the house.

A woman opened the door. She was about fifty years old, with wide brown eyes that made her seem girlish. She looked, John realised with a slight shock, somehow familiar.

"Yes?" she said gently. "What can I do for you?"

"Are you Mrs. Caldicott?" asked John, his pulse thudding.

"Yes . . ."

"Mrs. *Edna* Caldicott?"

"Yes . . ."

"Used to be Edna Thompson?"

"Yes . . . Now, what is all this?"

John hadn't thought about how he was going to explain himself. Now he was here, facing the girl—the woman—herself, he felt a little stupid.

"I—I think Tommy's been haunting me," he said awkwardly.

122

"Tommy?"

"Yes, Tommy. Leonard. Your brother. He's been playing tricks on me."

Mrs. Caldicott went pale and fiddled with the sparkling ring on her right hand. "Here," she said, "you'd better come in."

He told her the whole story. Sometimes she laughed and sometimes she looked puzzled. When he got to the end of it she looked solemn, as if remembering Tommy's death.

"Of course," she said when he had finished, "you realise it's all nonsense—well, some of it. I'll admit we did have a red front door, but all that stuff about Mrs. Gedge—well! She was *ever* so kind to us, specially when Mum and Dad died. But Tommy, oh, he could be a little devil. Used to say she was an ogress, that she ate boys and girls for supper. He loved a bit of drama. All that bit about cleaning drains was pure imagination. And as for calling him Leonard, well, he wouldn't give us any peace unless we did. He had some fanciful idea it made him sound better than the rest of us. He was always in trouble at school—used to go on about how he owned a horse and galloped over the Downs at night, that sort of thing. Oh no, dear."

John was confused. He didn't want to hear any more. He could no longer trust his own feelings. After all, he had *been* Tommy for a while, had suffered as Tommy had suffered. Or *had* Tommy suffered? Was John merely the victim of his own imagination? It didn't make sense.

"What about the ring?" he asked. "Why wasn't it in the box?"

Edna Caldicott laughed. "Because it never was—at least, not for long. Tommy told me where he'd put it, and I took it out again. Here it is." She held up her right hand, and the ring glistened richly. "But no diamonds, I'm afraid," she went on. "It's paste. Not worth more than a few pounds—a few shillings in those days, I expect. Typical Tommy, wanting to glamorise everything." She frowned. "But it's odd that he's still around that house.

Very odd," she added, looking sideways at John, as if she suspected him of being as untruthful as her brother.

John turned away. She didn't really believe him. Yet how did she explain the way he knew all about Tommy? He'd have to go home and fetch the exercise book, *then* she'd take him seriously.

"Now, dear," she was saying, "how about a piece of cake? I've got one in the kitchen—made from one of Mrs. Gedge's own recipes. How about that?" She stood up and went towards the door. As she reached it she turned and said thoughtfully: "You know, it's funny about that composition of yours. Tommy never learned to read or write."

John walked home lost in thought. Tommy couldn't write. And if he couldn't write, he couldn't have copied John's handwriting. So John must have written the story himself. But how? In his sleep? Had he done it unconsciously, so that he was unable to remember afterwards?

But Tommy must have been there, putting the words into his head, otherwise there would have been no box to find in the shed, no Edna. John *couldn't* have made it all up.

Anyway, he still had the book. He would take it to Mrs. Caldicott in the morning.

"Where've you been, then?" asked his father, as John dashed past him and ran up to his room.

Eagerly, John grabbed the exercise book and turned the pages. There it was, "My Home"—only the words were all John's own, even down to the green front door. All that Tommy had put into his mind was gone. There remained page after page of blank paper until, right at the end, he came across something quite out of place in an English Composition book.

John blinked in amazement and read:

Once I had a little pig
It really was a smasher,
And when it wagged its curly tail
It tickled its bacon rasher.

Crazy. Ridiculous. But yes, that sounded like Tommy

all right. John rubbed at the words, hoping they might disappear like the others, but they remained solid. He could see he'd have some job explaining them to Mr. Lawler. "How dare you deface school property!" He could just hear it.

Then some movement brought his eye back to the page, and, as he stared, he saw more words appearing, as if written by an invisible hand.

They said: *"Good joke, eh? Well, bye for now, mate. See yer around. L. Thompson (Tommy)."*

As this last word was formed, the laugh came again, only this time it seemed to drift away through the open window, across the building site towards the trees.

"See yer," said John, and found himself grinning.

BLACK HARVEST

by Ann Cheetham

A chilling story of terror and suspense...

The west coast of Ireland seems a perfect place for a family holiday — until everything begins to go horribly wrong...

Colin becomes aware of a ghastly stench from the land — a smell of death and decay... Prill is haunted by a fearsome skeleton-woman, who crawls through her dreams in hideous tormnt... Baby Alison falls sick with a sinister illness...

And their cousin Oliver? In those stiflingly hot summer days, as some nameless evil from the past closes in on them, Oliver remains unnaturally, unnervingly calm...

Armada

Nightmares

Bloodcurdling tales of gruesome terror!

Edited by Mary Danby

DON'T READ THIS BOOK…
If you're afraid of rats and spiders…. If you can't stand the sight of blood…. If you won't go to sleep with the wardrobe door open….

But if you're made of sterner stuff, dare yourself to try these fiendish horror tales — every one a nightmare of shuddersome fun!

Armada

CAPTAIN ARMADA

HI KIDS! I'VE GOT THE POWER TO BRING YOU FUN, ADVENTURE, AND EXCITEMENT!

Here are just a few of the best-selling titles that Armada has to offer:

- ☐ The Castle of Darkness *J.H. Brennan* £1.50
- ☐ Anyone Can Draw *Introduced by Tony Hart* £1.25
- ☐ The Funniest Funbook *Edited by Mary Danby* £1.25
- ☐ What Katy Did *Susan M. Coolidge* 95p
- ☐ A Fresh Wind in the Willows *Dixon Scott* £1.25
- ☐ Ten Ponies & Jackie *Judith M. Berrisford* £1.25
- ☐ The Mystery of the Scar-Faced Beggar
  Three Investigators Series £1.25
- ☐ The Emperor's Pony *Ann Sheldon* £1.25
- ☐ The Wizard of Oz *L. Frank Baum* 95p
- ☐ Little Men *Louisa M. Alcott* £1.25
- ☐ Shadow the Sheepdog *Enid Blyton* £1.25

Armadas are available in bookshops and newsagents, but can also be ordered by post.

HOW TO ORDER
ARMADA BOOKS, Cash Sales Dept., GPO Box 29, Douglas, Isle of Man. British Isles. Please send purchase price plus 15p per book (maximum postal charge £3·00). Customers outside the UK also send purchase price plus 15p per book. Cheque, postal or money order — no currency.

NAME (Block letters) _____

ADDRESS _____

_____

_____